Kitty's War

Daman Singh is the author of two previous novels, *Nine by Nine* (2008) and *The Sacred Grove* (2010), and three works of non-fiction, *The Last Frontier: People and Forests in Mizoram* (1996), *Strictly Personal* (2014), a memoir of her parents Manmohan Singh and Gursharan Kaur, and *Asylum: The Battle for Mental Healthcare in India* (2021). She lives in Delhi with her husband and dog.

DAMAN SINGH

First published by Tranquebar, an imprint of Westland Publications Private Limited, in 2018

Published by Tranquebar, an imprint of Westland Books, a division of Nasadiya Technologies Private Limited, in 2023

No. 269/2B, First Floor, 'Irai Arul', Vimalraj Street, Nethaji Nagar, Alapakkam Main Road, Maduravoyal, Chennai 600095

Westland, the Westland logo, Tranquebar and the Tranquebar logo are the trademarks of Nasadiya Technologies Private Limited, or its affiliates.

Copyright © Daman Singh, 2018

Daman Singh asserts the moral right to be identified as the author of this work.

ISBN: 9789357764735

10 9 8 7 6 5 4 3 2 1

This is a work of fiction. Names, characters, organisations, places, events and incidents are either products of the author's imagination or used fictitiously.

All rights reserved

Typeset in Adobe Jenson Pro by SÜRYA, New Delhi
Printed at Saurabh Printers Pvt. Ltd.

No part of this book may be reproduced, or stored in a retrieval system, or transmitted in any form or by any means, electronic, mechanical, photocopying, recording, or otherwise, without express written permission of the publisher.

1
Kitty

Kitty padded over to the window in her knitted socks. She opened it just a crack, but the cold knifed its way in anyhow. Not that she cared.

Once again she sat down on her trunk and once again it refused to close. This time her knickers were in the way. The peach ones edged with lace. The ones she wore when she saw Jonathan for the last time. She had thought it would be the first of many such times. It was not. The peach knickers stayed exactly where they were.

Jonathan was like that, never one to rush. At the annual school dance where they first met, she had sat out each number while her friends foxtrotted with the seniors from St Patrick's, not always keeping them at arm's length. By the time he finally introduced himself, the band was putting away their instruments. That was three years ago.

Everyone had known that Jonathan would top the Senior Cambridge exam. After that, it was simple for him to get into the training institute attached to the Jamalpur railway workshop, although it took just ten students a year. He was the only Anglo Indian in his class – the rest were all European. Most of the boys she knew did not make it to high school. Instead, they dropped out and joined the railways as a fitter, a cleaner, or an apprentice machinist. Next year, Jonathan would start off as an assistant mechanical engineer. He was brainy, everyone knew that. He was bound to do really well. He had a future. They had a future.

Not any more, though.

As she struggled to fold her dressing gown, Kitty was grateful for the knock on the door. It was Ester. Scrubbed and combed, she stood with her hands behind her back, feet planted wide apart.

'Kit – I mean, Miss Riddle –' she began.

'Term is over,' Kitty informed her coldly. 'You don't have to call me that now.'

Craning her neck, Ester peered into Kitty's room. 'Mr Marshall told me to tell you that the gharry will be here at half past nine to take you and I—'

'You and me. Or us.'

'But Mrs Peterson says that it's always—'

'Not always, but never mind.'

' To take you and I to the station,' Ester finished firmly.

Kitty shifted a little to the right to block Ester's view. 'Anything else?'

'Yes,' Ester said in her saucy way. 'Don't be late this time.'

Kitty stepped out into the corridor, but Ester was already skipping away in triumph. Kitty retreated.

For years she had pictured herself striding into a classroom of diligent little girls, filling their minds with nuggets of knowledge, gazing fondly at rows of heads bent over their lessons. It was pure luck that St Anne's had offered her a job as soon as she finished her training. And it had been lovely to be back as a teacher in her old school. The place was just as she remembered it. Except that the diligent little girls had been replaced with devious little devils. They had the upper hand, and knew it too. By the second term, she was completely wrung out. Exams had never bothered her as a student. As a teacher, she found them hell.

The school year was over at last, but the torture was not. She had promised to keep an eye on Ester Llewellyn. Which meant that she would be confined with her in a railway carriage all the way home to Pipli. There was no escape.

The dressing gown was waiting for her with outstretched arms.

Of late, Jonathan's letters were mostly about the war. If she did not know for a fact that he had been in Jamalpur all along, she would have assumed that they came from the front. It was as though newspapers and newsreels transported him to bloody battlefields across Europe. Last Christmas, he was supposed to have come to Pipli to meet her father. He wrote to say that he could not make it, not while London was being battered in the Blitz. Kitty was disappointed, but she knew what he meant. It was almost indecent to think about their future when people's lives were being ripped apart back home. She waited till September before bringing it up again. This time, it was the siege of Leningrad. The city was encircled, supplies were strangled, and the Russians were starving.

Everyone was disturbed by the war. There was horror, rage, fear. And guilt – for being safely out of its reach. Jonathan just needed a little more time, that was all. She was perfectly willing to wait. Once he had thought things through, he would show up in Pipli as planned. He was sure to make it this Christmas.

Twiddling with the knobs of the radio, she managed to coax it to life. It was too early for the news, but she listened to the disembodied voice anyway.

> Initial reports say that the first wave of between fifty and one hundred and fifty bombers pounded warships, aircraft and military installations at Pearl Harbor on Oahu, the third largest and chief island of Hawaii. It is believed that the surprise attack on the American naval base was launched from two aircraft carriers. Japan has declared war on Britain and the United States.

Nothing made sense any more, not since Jonathan's telegram had arrived a day ago. Kitty sat down and burst into tears. Beneath her, the trunk snapped shut.

They were late after all. It was not her fault. After they waved to Mr Marshall and the last of the remaining staff and students, the gharry-wallah discovered that one of the horses was missing a shoe. He refused to leave without first searching the driveway. By the time they got to the station, the train was already on the platform. The ticket collector glanced at their faces and hurried them through, barking at the sea of brown to part. Their coolie sailed forth like a camel, both trunks perched high on his head. The carriage for Europeans and Anglo Indians was further down. A railway constable stood by to keep others out. A native boy rushed past, holding a small goat slung over his shoulder. Within seconds, he was swallowed up by the mass of humans squeezing its way into the third-class coaches up ahead. The engine wheezed and the frantic cries of tea-sellers filled the air. Kitty breathed in the sticky smokiness and pushed Ester aboard.

After that, she simply surrendered. To the silhouette of the mountains that stayed, no matter which way the train turned. To the streaks of sunlight that flashed through the open windows. To the perfume of pine that lingered long after the landscape began to flatten. To the sight of Ester demolishing three marmalade sandwiches without a serviette on her lap.

As the murmur of unfamiliar voices floated by, she sensed that they were no longer alone. An English couple was conversing pleasantly in low tones. Their luggage looked shiny and new, just like them. Without warning, the train lurched and a half-eaten apple landed at her feet. The English couple stopped talking. Ester jumped down from the upper berth, retrieved the apple, and dropped it in the dustbin. Ascending to her perch again, she bumped her head against the roof of the carriage with a loud thud. The lady in the tiny hat continued to read her book and the gentleman continued to read his newspaper. They could well have been sitting by the fireplace in their private salon, instead of hurtling through the Indian countryside in a first-class carriage shared with two nameless strangers.

The polite thing to do would have been to introduce herself, but Kitty did not wish to intrude. All this while, she had been slumped in a corner like a sack of potatoes. Now she sat up straight and crossed her ankles neatly, wishing that her skirt was less creased and her hair less rumpled. This time the gentleman did look up, but he lowered his gaze almost immediately.

The attendant came to take their order for lunch at the next station. It was Alfred. He was already old when she went up to St Anne's for the first time. Now he wore spectacles and walked with a slight stoop. She opened her mouth to ask how he was, but he had turned to the lady in the tiny hat. After he finished describing the ingredients in every dish on the menu, the lady ordered cucumber sandwiches. Alfred jotted that down and winked at Kitty, who decided that she was not hungry. Ester, however, was.

The next time she opened her eyes, they were alone again. Curled up under a light blanket, Ester looked quite harmless. Her tuck box was lying on the folding table. Kitty picked it up cautiously. The blanket did not stir. She opened the box and looked inside. It was empty. Bitterly, she placed it back on the table. The train did not have a restaurant car. Orders for meals were telegraphed to the next junction station. The next junction was Pipli.

As the metal wheels clattered hollowly over a bridge, the door of the attached bathroom swung open. Kitty crossed over and gave it a kick. The spacious compartment felt suddenly cramped, its air sour and stale. Alfred must have closed the windows before he left. She raised the glass panes as well as the wire gauze screens – in any case, it was too late in the year for mosquitoes. At once, the limp curtains leapt to life, flailing about helplessly in the cold night breeze. Bending to peer out into the inky blackness, she fingered the grey linen, rubbing her thumb against the woven insignia. Absently, she plucked at a loose thread. An entire elephant vanished before she knew what was happening.

2
Terrence

Terrence Riddle set down his glass and went inside to turn up the volume. As he settled back in his cane chair, the wistful melody mingled with the meditative chirp of crickets. The combination was surprisingly pleasing.

That morning, he had set off in the push trolley soon after daybreak. A keyman had reported loose bolts on his beat the previous evening. The passenger train was not due till early afternoon and repairs on the branch line were to be completed before that. There was a nip in the air and the ground was still drizzled with dew. By the time the tracks entered open country, the sun's rays were beating down on his khaki sola topee.

Stanley McBride and his men had been waiting for him at the site. The flags were already set up and the bolts lubricated. The mate signalled to a gangman to remove a set of eight fishplates. Terrence examined each with a magnifying glass before handing them one by one to Stan. They were in good shape, which was fortunate because stocks were running low and supplies had been held up for weeks. The bolts, however, would have to be replaced. It was not uncommon for the threads to wear out, so he ruled out foul play. Although one could never be too sure these days.

Walking down the ganglength, Terrence stopped to watch the labourers clear the tall grass that was closing in on the embankment. Left uncut, it could weaken the ballast, quite apart from posing a serious fire hazard. Aware of his gaze, the men swung their scythes faster. Blades glinted in the sun and whistled through the air. He was not the only one looking on – two village women squatted a short distance away, no doubt hoping to gather the grass once it was cut. Terrence left instructions to allow this, and moved on.

Further away, the track curved left before covering the last mile to the next wayside station. He cursed as his ankle-length boot caught on a jagged stone, causing him to stumble. Although the sleepers were anchored securely, the ballast was freshly disturbed. Hearing a rustle beneath the trees, he stopped. Despite the scanty rains that year, the undergrowth was high enough to hide someone who wished to remain unseen. Then he relaxed as a wild boar shot through a gap in the bushes. It must have been alarmed by the workers on the line. Wild boar were fairly common in the area. It was breeding season, and a sow with her litter could be a nasty piece of work. Swinging his sturdy walking stick, Terrence had turned around and gone back the way he had come.

At the opening notes of the allegretto, his eyes closed and his fingers followed the movement as it lightened and lifted. It would soon give way to a tempest of rippling arpeggios, each more masterful than the last. Before this could happen, a shadow blocked the doorway. It was Kitty. He should have asked her to join him in the verandah – normally he did. But it was late by the time he finished checking the registers that had been put up for inspection that day. Besides, he had simply forgotten that she was home for the holidays.

Kitty sat down on the steps and slipped off her sandals. As she leaned forward to prop her chin in her cupped hands, her chestnut curls hid her face from him. For a while, neither of them moved. Then his left hand rose as if in a trance and chopped up the air between them in short, swift strokes. Scratching noisily, the needle reached the end of the gramophone record. As if on cue, a small white dog slid out from under his chair, picked her way delicately across the lawn and left through the front gate.

'She only comes for the music,' Terrence clarified, 'though I'm surprised she sat through *Midnight Sonata*. She doesn't much care for Beethoven.'

Kitty did not comment. She did not much care for dogs. But for her, he would have had half a dozen about the house. The white dog had first dropped by a few months back. She did not wish to move in, nor did she wish to be fed. Terrence saw no harm in having her over on the odd evening. Kitty would get over it. In any case, she was leaving in March when the new term began.

'Couldn't sleep, poppet?'

Kitty shrugged.

'Feeling all right? You look a bit peaky. Shall I ring for Ayah?'

'I'm fine.' Her voice creaked, as if it had not been used in a very long time.

'Hungry?'

Kitty did not reply. She was gazing intently at the fireflies chasing each other above the lilies.

'Shall I make you some cocoa then?'

As he observed the back of Kitty's head, Terrence realised that he had barely spoken with his daughter since she came home. He left for work right after breakfast. Lunch was brought to his office these days. By the time he was back for supper, she had gone to bed. It was a busy time for him. Last month, he had been laid low by malaria and the paperwork had piled up. Progress reports, estimates for new works and stock inventories lay unfinished on his desk. Once the Christmas spirit took hold of them, it would be difficult to collar the men. Some of the younger ones were already showing signs of merriment. He found this most annoying. They were perfectly free to play the fool after hours and, by all accounts, they did. The Pipli Railway Institute – a fancy name for the club – might not boast a swimming pool and tennis courts as did the larger railway colonies, but it did have a bar, a billiards room, card tables and a dance floor.

Not that any of this was of the slightest interest to

him. There used to be a time when sundown would find him at the institute, invariably steering his partner to a grand slam in whist. He had quite a reputation in those days, and it followed him from one posting to the next.

The catering was dodgy in some places, but the bar was always first rate. Dances he avoided like the plague. They carried on till the early hours of the morning and he was the sort who needed his sleep. But he could always be persuaded to play the piano for the band, just a couple of numbers to get the party started. The opening bars of *The Entertainer* would have everyone dashing to the floor. Before they had a chance to catch their breath, he would plunge into *Bill Bailey, Won't You Please Come Home* – just a tad faster than Lorraine Foreman and The Singing Waiters sang it. He would leave soon after, but not without playing *Fascination* for all those amorous couples who could wait no longer to dance close.

That was a long time ago. At some point, he had stopped going altogether. The colony swarmed with children of all sizes and it was perfectly safe to send Kitty with her friends. When she was old enough to go for the weekly dance, Betty Bolton told him that he must chaperone her. He did not. There were plenty of ladies who took it upon themselves to keep an eye on every girl in the room. Boys who misbehaved were promptly booted out – he had first-hand experience of this. Besides, Kitty could look after herself.

Terrence decided to fix himself another drink. While he was inside, he removed the record from the turntable, wiped it carefully, and slipped it into its sleeve. When he returned, Kitty was still sitting on the steps, her hair tucked behind her ears. He sat down next to her and put an arm around her waist. She had been seven when she left for boarding school. Since then, he had only seen her for three months in a year. It always took him a while to get used to her being home. This time it was taking longer than usual. He must be getting old.

'Remember the new railway line to Giridih? We started laying it last winter. Work stopped after you left. Now it looks like we can get on with it. Everything is in place, we're just waiting for the final go-ahead from headquarters.'

'Good,' she said without enthusiasm.

'Did you notice the new high-power lamps at the station? And that the platform has been raised? You mustn't have had to jump far this time.'

'No, I didn't.'

He could not tell whether she had not seen the high-power lamps, or whether she did not have to jump far. Regardless, he carried on. 'I saw young Jimmy the other day. He asked about you.'

'Oh?'

'There isn't a single sensible thought in that head of his. I caught him fooling around with the hoses at the siding.'

Kitty was a good judge of character. She was far too smart to waste her time dilly-dallying with some boy, especially one as witless as Jimmy.

'Edmund Dobbs was transferred to Asansol on promotion,' he continued. 'You knew them, didn't you? There's a new assistant stationmaster in place of Dobbs.'

'I knew their daughter Mindy. She was all right. We started a band – Emily, Mindy and I. The Skylarks. Emily and I sang, Mindy mostly bleated along. Jimmy was our manager. Have they left already?'

Terrence said that they had.

'Who's the new chap? Is he nice?'

'Nice enough, I reckon. We haven't had a native officer before, but he should do just fine.'

Kitty took this in. 'Really? A native? What's his name?'

He gulped down the rest of his whisky before answering.

Kitty frowned thoughtfully. 'Chuckerbutty? How very odd.'

3
Kitty

The naked girl in the mirror parted her lips and tried to smile. The result was pathetic. She ran her tongue over her teeth and tried again. This time it was a bit better. Raking a hand through her damp curls, she let them fall about her face. If only they were longer in front. Then nobody would notice that her eyes were puffy. Jonathan used to say they were green, not blue. Jonathan said a lot of things.

She blew her nose, far too hard. But it hurt less than the jagged blade that was lodged inside her stomach. She took a deep breath and counted till a hundred, it was supposed to help. Sometimes it really did. But not this time.

The banging on the door resumed. Kitty climbed into her steamy underwear, hauled a bright floral printed dress over her head and thrust her arms through its puff sleeves. Emily flinched when she saw her emerge. 'Lovely,' she said brightly, 'now let's go.'

Kitty did not want to go anywhere, but Emily's mother was anxious to see her. Mrs Llewellyn fussed about, producing a tray of homemade fruit cake, rose cookies and fudge, and a tall glass of fizzy lemonade. Her great-grandmother was French and she did not let anybody forget this. Kitty felt obliged to eat her way across the tray as Emily flipped through a stack of *Woman & Home*.

'Here, this is it.' Emily pushed the magazine at her, stabbing the open page with her forefinger. 'What d'you say?'

Kitty studied the elegant burgundy crepe-de-chine gown. 'Perfect,' she mumbled through the last piece of fudge. 'But how?'

'Simple. Mum bought the cloth and beads from Calcutta. She and Mrs Mascarenhas went there for Christmas shopping. The durzi from Pipli said he could easily copy the pattern. He's going to sit and sew it in the back verandah.'

Kitty pointed out that the New Year's ball was just two weeks away.

'It won't take him more than two days – three at the most – there's plenty of time. What are you wearing?'

'Don't worry about me,' Kitty said, 'I'm not going.'

'Don't be silly. Of course you're going. Everyone goes.'

'Well, not this one.'

Emily snorted.

'I mean it, Em, I'm not.'

Emily gave her an appraising look. 'Did you and Jonathan fight?'

Kitty covered her mouth politely and coughed.

'So you did fight. I thought so. Hiding at home for days on end, wearing 1920s frocks, not shaving your legs, finishing all the fudge—'

'That's not fair,' Kitty protested.

The door opened and Ester's head appeared. Emily told her younger sister to get out.

Kitty waited for the door to close before reaching for a rose cookie.

'So,' Emily continued, 'what happened?'

'Nothing. Nothing happened. It's just – over.'

Emily widened her eyes. 'He ditched you!'

'I didn't say that.' It was annoying that Emily should instantly reach this conclusion.

'What! You ditched him! Don't tell me!'

'I wasn't going to,' Kitty said truthfully.

'But why?'

Kitty sighed weakly. 'It's just this stupid war, it changed everything—'

'What rubbish!'

'Well, I can't come up with a better reason.'

Emily could. 'Look, I always knew he was wrong for you. I know I didn't say it, but I knew it all along. Jonathan's a sweet chap, but he's so bloody serious. You're not like that, not one bit.'

That was not true. Jonathan could be a lot of fun. As a matter of fact, he was excellent at ping pong. Besides, she could be serious too. Not that Emily would know.

'Opposites attract in the beginning, but it never

lasts – take it from me.' She paused thoughtfully. 'He's a lot like your father, isn't he? They say a girl's first beau is either exactly like her father, or the exact opposite.'

Kitty found this disturbing. Then she remembered that Jonathan was not her first beau – Jimmy was.

Emily was contrite now. 'Poor you, no wonder you look so awful. Let's not talk about it, it's much too soon. Come and see the darling curtains that Mum picked up in Cal.' She took Kitty gently by the arm and led her out of the room.

Mrs Llewellyn was coming down the hallway with a plate of freshly baked scones. Kitty said she could not possibly eat any more. Mrs Llewellyn was not one to give up so easily. She hurried back to the kitchen to fetch a tin for Kitty to take home with her.

The corridor was decorated with photographs of several generations of Llewellyns and Furnells. Some frames were old and chipped, the images yellowed or faded. But most were in surprisingly good shape, neatly inscribed with names, places and dates. Originally from Wales and Normandy respectively, the two families had certainly travelled – and not just to Bombay, Calcutta and Madras. Their itinerary included Poona, Waltair, Jubbalpore, Allahabad, Rajahmundry, Cawnpore, Gooty, Lillooah – and Jamalpur, of course.

An 1823 painting presided over the display. It was the portrait of a gentleman in regimentals, sporting bushy sideburns and a gimlet gaze. Below him were various pictures of men in various kinds of uniform – military to begin with, but mostly civilian as the decades went by. Kitty skipped these – they all looked the same to her. In a family scene, four mustachioed men posed in bow ties and ill-fitting suits, while five solemn ladies sat buttoned up to the chin. A group of children were at their first holy communion, the girls in white frocks charmingly rounded off with veils and wreaths of flowers in their hair. The little boys wore smart blazers, their arms obediently folded for the camera. Further on, a victorious hockey team in shirts and shapeless shorts proudly held their sticks across their chests. One of them was left-handed; his stick stopped just short of the next player's ear. A stout lady in a long gown was holding a rifle upright, one foot placed squarely on a dead bear. To her right, a dreamy young man with delicate features leaned lazily against a picket fence.

The three heads encased in tight swimming caps bobbing about in a pool marked the beginning of a new era. By this time, every other photograph included a locomotive, carriage or wagon. Styles had changed. Four young ladies sat in identical pleated dresses with Chelsea collars. Their shapely legs were crossed at the same angle, their identical pumps pointed in the same direction. A bashful Mr Llewellyn and a spritely Miss Furnell held hands and brandished tennis rackets. Not long after that, they stood outside a church, duly wedded. Two ayahs – heads covered and feet bare – held one Llewellyn offspring each, while two older children pressed close by their sides. Ester was one of the infants.

The other, Eugene, had died of typhoid. Despite her starched pinafore apron and nurse's cap, Emily looked like a film star. Her tightly belted waist appeared absurdly small. Kitty stepped up to get a closer look. Emily was sucking in her breath for sure.

Every railway family preserved its photographs and put them on display. But there were no such relics from the Riddles' past. The trunk in which they had been packed was lost in transit somewhere between Gomoh and Son Nagar, years ago. At least, that was what her father claimed. Personally, she believed he had got rid of them because they reminded him of her mother.

Leaving the Llewellyns' armed with a tin of scones, Kitty was in no particular hurry to get home. She strolled down the lane, stopping to admire the wild roses climbing the trellis in the Pritchet garden. A gang of children raced by on bicycles with hoots and howls. One boy zigzagged ahead and dived headlong into a hedge. Old Mr Morris climbed shakily out of his hammock and ticked him off roundly. Unhurt, the boy took off at top speed.

Kitty stopped to say hello. On her last visit home, she had tea with the Morrises. All Morris men were in the railways and all Morris girls married railwaymen. Old Mr Morris lived with his son. He had droned on about his days as 'Madman Morris', the intrepid mail-train driver. He did not seem to recognise her now. When she told him her name, he said he knew she was 'that Riddle girl' and asked how the baby was. His mind was clearly wandering.

The black-and-white images of Emily's mammoth family were reminders of its colourful past. There was so much blending of blood – English, Welsh, French, Portuguese, Dutch and, according to Mrs Llewellyn's diligent research, Danish as well. Somewhere along the way, the early settlers from Europe had married native women. So Indian blood had obviously blended in too. But Mrs Llewellyn did not know anything about that bit. The only natives in her story were servants. Like the two ayahs – heads covered and feet bare.

Guts, grit and glory dominated the tales of times past. But there were also vile acts of betrayal and ghastly scenes of violence. The dreamy young man with delicate features, for instance, had been dragged from his house and slaughtered in front of his wife and two little children. Their native servants had let the killers in. This kind of thing had happened to many people at many places during the Indian Sepoy Mutiny of 1857.

By the time Kitty got home, the tin of scones was considerably lighter. She handed it to Latif, who was furiously pounding spices for ball curry and yellow rice. As she drifted back to her room, she wondered whether he would have opened that door.

4
Ayah

She hurried into the bathroom. Miss Kitty's dressing gown was hanging behind the door. Sahib was right. It smelled bad. Briskly, she stripped the bed, changed the sheets and folded the quilt neatly, all the while listening for the sound of chairs scraping back in the dining room. When they did, she swooped down on the pile of clothes on the floor and bundled them up. The front door slammed. Sahib had left for work.

As soon as she had tucked the bundle under her arm, Miss Kitty wandered in and collapsed facedown on the bed. She thought of telling her not to lie down so soon after eating, but decided against it. After all, she was not her mother. She closed the door gently behind her and went to the kitchen.

Latif was humming tunelessly to himself amidst the clatter of pots and pans. He did not look up as she left through the pantry door. Her slippers were lying on the step, next to Latif's much bigger ones. She made her way through the back lanes of the colony, stopping now and then to chat with a passer-by. Ayahs, cooks, gardeners, dhobis, sweepers – she knew them all. She knew the sahibs and memsahibs too – by house number, not by name.

The memsahib in C-3 had six cats. She kept a cow specially for them.

When the B-21 sahib had too much to drink, he climbed up on the red tiled roof and sang loudly. A few months ago, he had fallen off and broken his arm.

Pipli water did not suit the memsahib in B-4. She was always sick, poor thing. The B-4 sahib was very worried about her. They only ate boiled food – no oil, no masala, not even haldi. Haldi would have been good for her.

C-6 always smelled of paint. The older boy did not let anybody into his room, only the sweeper. The people in his paintings wore very few clothes. His father kept shouting at him to get a job.

In all these years, Sahib had never shouted at her. She had come to work at B-15 after the family in A-3 left for Bhagalpur. On the second day, while tidying his room, she saw that the small almirah by his bed was open. She tried to close it, but a hinge was loose, so the shutters would not come together. Sahib had walked in just then. His eyes were angry, but he did not shout. She would not have minded if he had. If a man cannot shout in his own house, where can he? From that day, the almirah was always locked.

Sahib was a good man. He did not poke his nose here

and there. He let her work the way she knew. Sometimes he gave her things – a jar of jam, socks, an umbrella. This morning, he had handed her an orange. Also, he spoke nicely, in proper Hindi. It was hard to understand what the other sahibs said. Miss Kitty spoke proper Hindi too, though not nicely. But it did not matter. She would soon be gone.

After leaving the dirty clothes with the dhobi, Ayah walked to the main gate of the colony, greeting the chowkidar as he opened it for her. Circling the boundary wall, she picked her way through straggling bushes till she reached the gravel road leading to the goods yard.

The men were on the other side of the culvert, about a dozen of them, sitting and smoking bidis. As Ayah walked up, one of them pointed to a figure stretched out in the shade of a babul tree.

An arm flung across his eyes, shirt rolled under his head, the young man was asleep. Ayah cleared away the twigs and leaves, then sat down and prepared to wait. His burnished chest was taut and smooth. She put out a hand as if to stroke it. He sat up just then and was instantly wide awake.

Reaching for the end of her sari, Ayah untied the orange and gave it to him. He peeled it and held it out to her, but she did not want any. After he tossed the peel into the bushes, she asked if there was any news.

He shook his head. 'No, nothing.'

Ayah picked up a leaf and tore it into small pieces. 'Maybe the others have—'

'See, if I hear something, I'll tell you myself.' He put on his shirt and wiped his sticky hands on it. 'I tell you, it's a good thing he left. That time, they said the work will go on, so I stayed. But now it's over. That's what I heard.'

'He should have waited. I told him to wait. He didn't listen. You should wait.'

'How long? I can't wait any more. There's nothing for me here. In a few days I will go.'

'To Mitali?'

By now, the maize must have been dried in the sun. A portion was always set aside for seed. The rest was ground into flour, bit by bit, for a few days at a time. When a child was born, the mother ate a gruel of maize to make more milk. In a good year, the maize would last maybe two, or even three, months of the cold season. It filled the stomach, but it did not taste as good as rice. Nothing tasted as good as the rice from the fields of her village. All the menfolk would return to Mitali when it was time to harvest.

'No,' he said, interrupting her thoughts, 'to Raneegunge.'

Ayah gazed at his boyish face. It would soon become harsh and unforgiving. The coal mine did that. It sucked out all that was good and kind and spat out the remains – men without souls. They came back wasted in body and spirit, too feeble to be of much use at home. They came with anger, bitterness and empty pockets. And lashed out at whatever – or whoever – was around. Some left for the mine, again and again. Some never came back, ever.

She got to her feet and dusted down her sari. 'Tell me before you go,' she said, and left without saying goodbye to the others.

Trudging along the tracks, Ayah looked straight ahead, unmindful of the shrieking whistle of the express. When it was almost upon her, she stepped aside to let the metal monster pass. Although the engine was yet to pick up speed, the passengers' faces were blurred, distorted. After the last bogie had rolled by, she walked on. Somewhere in the distance, it was raining. Dark clouds hovered over the low hills in the north, their edges melting into shades of purple. Wisps of pale mauve twirled out across the sky before being swallowed up by the vast sweep of sheer blue. With a splash of showy wing, a neelkanth dropped down upon an unwary insect, carrying it off to the telegraph wire overhead. She stopped to watch, shielding her eyes from the sun. Then, having lost her sense of direction, she simply followed the railway tracks wherever they led her. When she found herself in a clearing of ber trees, she realised that she had come too far.

Retracing her steps, she took a path turning right. Filtered by leaves, the sun was on her back now, soft and warm. As the tightness in her head began to ease, Ayah undid her long black hair and shook it loose, before winding it up again. The path forked at the marshalling yard. She was not supposed to cut across but she did, making it to the other end without being noticed.

Outside the archway of the station entrance was an old banyan tree. A tonga stood in its shade, its owner nowhere to be seen. The horse stretched his neck towards her and quivered his lower lip. Beyond the banyan was the post office. Its door was closed but not bolted.

They had already sorted the mail. She saw it lying in neat piles on the long table. The older man was placing them in pigeonholes, the corners of his mouth reddened by betel juice. The younger one was slurping tea from a small earthen cup.

'Oy! Look what you did!'

Ayah started guiltily, but the older man was not talking to her. He took an envelope from one pile and placed it on top of a different one. Looking up, he saw her and shook his head.

'What!' he said in mock exasperation. 'You again!'

The younger man turned and told her to come back later. She ignored him. Kneeling, she picked up a letter that had slipped to the floor and placed it on the table.

'Couldn't wait for the postman? Everyone is in a hurry these days. Rush, rush, rush. As if the world is coming to an end. Tell me, sister, is it really?' Without waiting for an answer, he picked up a stack of letters. 'Let me see ... Korkat, Majra, Pipli, Pipli junction, here we are ... Pipli railway colony. A-15, no?'

'B-15,' she corrected, knowing that this was just a game he liked to play.

'Nothing,' he said with an exaggerated sigh.

Ayah's face crumpled, she could not help it. 'Nothing? Are you sure? Please look once again.'

He looked again and slapped his forehead with his palm. 'Of course! Here you are, sister. Forgive my mistake.'

Something inside her swelled at his words. Stepping forward, she took the bulky envelope from his outstretched hand, thanked him and hurried to the door.

'Mrs Ruby Bannister – that is your name, no?'

The younger man sniggered and tossed the empty cup out of the window with a practised hand.

Ayah walked back, put the envelope on the table, turned around and left.

5
Kitty

Thursday was movie night at the institute. Last week, they had screened *The Adventures of Robin Hood*. Kitty had walked out after the first half. She liked Errol Flynn, but he looked ridiculous prancing around in green tights. This week was *Gone with the Wind*. It had been all the rage ever since its release two years ago. The London magazines had given it lavish reviews and made much of the fact that Vivien Leigh was British. The girls of Pipli railway colony claimed her as their own, for she was born in Darjeeling, no more than 300 miles away. And those among them – Kitty and Emily included – who went to school in that very town had an intimate bond with the star.

She got there early to get a good seat. So did everybody else. Emily had saved a place for her in front, but Mrs Snow refused to vacate it. Kitty made her way to the back, wedging herself between Jennifer Willoughby and Mrs Morgan.

Before the movie started, there was a short feature about women in Britain, who were hard at work to win the war. After all, everyone had to do their bit. It opened with row upon row of them toiling in a factory. At the end of her shift, one emerged belting her trench coat, weary but fulfilled. She held out her arms as if to embrace the Royal Air Force bombers streaking across the red sky. In another scene, a girl in breeches and boots – her auburn curls tied back with a bright yellow ribbon – leaned on a pitchfork and gazed with pride at miles of golden fields.

Jennifer gave her a nudge. 'Looks just like Mindy, doesn't she?'

Kitty did not reply. Jonathan liked her hair untied. Like a lion's mane, he said. Damn him.

A grandmother, a mother and a daughter in gaily coloured aprons marched up to a row of garbage cans placed in an alley. A black terrier hastily scuttled out of their way. The grandmother dropped a bundle of waste paper into the first. The mother put an armful of scrap metal into the second. The daughter emptied a bunch of bones into the third. All this material would – somehow or the other – go to make ships, planes, tanks, guns and ammunition. There were murmurs of disbelief all around. At dinner time, a cheerful housewife cut thrifty slices of bread for her family, and saved the rest of the loaf for the next day. Under her watchful eye, not a morsel of the meal was chucked out. After clearing the table, she sat by a lamp and darned her husband's trousers. War, she declared, was a time to make do and mend. This was followed by the appearance of a pretty blonde in a red polka-dotted headscarf. She raised one eyebrow, flexed the muscles of her right arm and said that they could do it too. The feature came to an end with the message 'Keep Calm and Carry On' inscribed in big letters across the screen. To the patriotic residents of Pipli railway colony, this last message made perfect sense. Everybody clapped with gusto.

Apart from a few titters during the love scenes, the audience sat spellbound through the four-hour film. There was a good amount of sniffing, and many a hand clutched a soggy hanky. When the lights came on, Kitty looked around for Emily. She was chatting with some girls behind the snacks counter. It was one of her last evenings at Pipli before leaving for the base hospital at Ranchi. Kitty circled the group but could not find a way in. With a mute wave, she left.

The January air was chilly and she shivered a little as she walked the short distance home. At the front gate, she stopped for a while, wishing there was someplace else to go. Unable to think of any, she lifted the latch and went inside.

Later that night, she was restless for no particular reason. At first her quilt was too heavy, stifling her with its massive weight. Then it was too small, leaving her toes sticking out in the cold. Finally she made peace with it and drifted off to sleep. But a spasm in her left leg woke her up. She sat up in bed and squeezed the muscles in her calf. Once her leg stopped twitching, her stomach began to growl, louder by the minute. Flinging back the covers, she dashed to the pantry and fetched a tin of biscuits. By the time she was through with it, her quilt was too heavy again.

Now resigned to lying awake, her thoughts went back to the film. The American Civil War left her cold. But, like everyone else, she was mesmerised by Scarlett O'Hara's fiery spirit and exquisite gowns, Rhett Butler's sardonic drawl and cavalier ways. Those smouldering glances, those scorching kisses. Their love was so wilful, so wily. And completely oblivious of all that lay destroyed in its wake. Very romantic, no doubt. Still, a bit much.

Another thought was nagging at her, but she could not put a finger on it. It surfaced just before dawn. Why on earth had the Wilkeses named their poor daughter 'India'?

In the old days, she had seen Jimmy virtually every evening. She asked him home, but he was nervous of her father. Most people were. He would wait for her at the end of the lane and they strolled about the colony or sat on a kerb in the lamplight. Sometimes they went to his place and Emily, Daniel and Pat joined them there. Between horsing around, Jimmy would pluck the strings of his guitar and make them guess the song. Dan played bass to his lead, his hair brushing against the frets as he jiggled his head to the beat. Emily was undoubtedly the diva, holding her notes longer than anyone else could. After a few bars, Pat would pitch in with her husky contralto. They could spend hours like that, until Mr Mascarenhas told them to go away and let him get some sleep.

That evening, they met at the institute. The boys were having beer and Pat asked for a port and lemon. Kitty had a shandy. Em did not drink. If she had told the others about Jonathan, they did not let on. There were no awkward silences, no pitying looks. As usual, Dan was the butt of all their jokes, not that he minded.

Fortified by four beers, Jimmy insisted on walking her home, casually suggesting that they take the back gate. There was no sign of her father. Kitty closed the door of her room and sat down on the bed. Jimmy took off his jacket and studied it closely. A tap was dripping in the bathroom, each plop a reminder of life passing her by. As the minutes ticked away, she realised that Jimmy was leaning towards her, inch by inch. She straightened up so that his lips could find hers. There was nothing worse than a last minute fumble. Just as his nose was level with hers, the door opened. Jimmy lurched forward and his startled lips landed on Kitty's left shoulder. She happened to be wearing a prickly woollen jumper that day.

Ayah went into the bathroom. After much clanging about, she emerged with a bucket and left without closing the door. She had not bothered to turn off the tap. It continued to drip as before.

Ayah had been behaving strangely of late. Sometimes she did not even reply when addressed. There were days when she crept about the house, picking things up and putting them down exactly where they had been. At other times, she flicked her duster viciously, sending feathers flying in all directions. It was hard to find things these days. A jar of pickles had been discovered on the shoe rack while Kitty's missing slippers ended up in the pantry. Entering her room without knocking was just the latest in a long list of misdemeanours.

Other people were behaving strangely too. A couple of weeks ago, Dan had taken the train to Allahabad to buy a second-hand motorcycle from a captain in the army cantonment. He rode it back, stopping at Pipli town on the last stretch. Pipli was more like a big village than a town. The market consisted mostly of a row of natives squatting on mats upon which they spread their wares, just as happy to barter as to sell. Dan had parked his bike under a tree and gone to fetch water because the engine was overheated. When he got back, both tyres were flat, somebody had let out the air. He had to wheel the bike all the way home.

The story had made them laugh, Jimmy the loudest. It was just the kind of prank he liked to play. The strange thing was that no native would have dared do anything like that in the past. Something had changed.

Maybe Ayah had changed too. When Kitty suggested this to her father, he told her not to be silly.

Kitty hunched over her scrambled egg, occasionally poking it with a fork. She took a bite of toast and chewed it for a very long time before swallowing it with a gulp of tea.

'So,' her father said, 'what are you doing today?'

'Nothing,' she replied.

'Nothing? Surely you have things to do?'

'Like what?' she asked.

To that he had no answer. 'Well, no harm in taking it easy. The holidays will be over before you know it. May as well make the most of them before school opens.'

'I'm not going back. Don't you know the job was only for one year?'

'One year to begin with. But then you wrote that Sister Veronica asked you to stay on.'

Kitty pushed her plate away and slid lower in her chair. 'She did. I didn't accept.'

'You didn't accept! Why didn't you accept?'

'I forgot.'

The furrow on his forehead deepened. 'You forgot!'

There were other things on her mind at the time. Jonathan, mostly.

'Well,' her father said, 'you can always accept the offer now.'

'No, I can't. It's too late.' She had been filling in for Mrs Henley, who was then laid up at the King Edward VII Sanatorium in Bhowali. Nobody had expected her to get better, but she did. Her telegram had arrived just before the final exams. She would be back at St Anne's the next term. Which was why Kitty would not.

Her father stood up and looked down at her anxiously. If he found this hard to swallow, it was a good thing she had not told him about Jonathan. He would never have understood.

'What you need is to get out of the house—'

'And go where?'

'I don't know, somewhere, anywhere. And for god's sake, get rid of that wretched dressing gown.'

6
Chuckerbutty

'The situation is tragic, very tragic.'

The young man behind the desk tapped his fountain pen as though flicking ash from it. The conversation had gone on far too long. He shifted in his chair, crossed and uncrossed his legs, and coughed repeatedly. Anything more than that would be seen as disrespect.

'Management must be more sensitive. Do you know he has five children? That his mother passed away not long ago?'

'Yes, Kailashji, I know all that. But this khalasi was found drinking on duty, not once but three times this month. Twice he was let off with a warning. It is out of my hands now.'

The union representative showed no signs of leaving. 'A poor man drowns his sorrows in liquor. What else can he do? Does his wretched life give him any other option?'

'I do see your point, Kailashji. But you are thinking only about one life, we have to think about many.'

Kailash Sahu folded his hands. 'Chakravarty babu, I too am thinking of many, I too. If one worker is dismissed, won't the other workers be upset? These are difficult times, are they not? We don't want to upset the men – who knows what ideas will get into their heads? Today they may be quiet, tomorrow they won't.'

'Today if one is let off for drunkenness, tomorrow ten will turn up drunk. We can't allow such indiscipline. Rules are rules. Action must be taken. Please try to understand my position.'

'Who said anything about rules? I am all for following rules. All I am saying is, let us show the poor man a little compassion, a little humanity. Put in a word for him, that's all I ask. Surely stationmaster sahib will listen to you.' Kailash Sahu stood up to go. 'One day we will be running the railways together, will we not? You help us now, we'll help you then. And the way this train is moving, that stop may come sooner than you think.'

Pulok Chakravarty smiled. It was no secret that Indians would be at the helm one day. But the railways ran – and very well too – according to established procedures and norms. Undermining the system would do no good, neither before India became free, nor after. A man as small-minded as Kailash Sahu would never understand this.

Ramaswami came in with a file and waited for the other man to leave before placing it on the assistant stationmaster's desk. Pulok lit a cigarette and wished the chief trains clerk had come in sooner instead of listening outside the door.

Pulok had been in Pipli for just over three months. It was his first posting. As a boy in Calcutta, he had spent all his free time at the Howrah railway station. It was not the machines that drew him there, it was the men. Officers in smart uniforms strode importantly about the platform, making sure everything was in order. Within minutes of a train coming to a halt, workmen climbed up on its roof to fill water in the overheated tanks. Others walked down its length, tapping each wheel with a handle as they went. The train examiner would have already set up the two red discs at either end of the platform. He handed one set of instructions to the engine driver at the head and the second set to the guard at the tail end. The guard stood outside the brake van, supervising the loading and unloading of parcels. Wagons were detached and led to the marshalling yard. The shunting master and pointsmen directed them through a maze of criss-crossing lines.

It was never enough for him to watch from an overbridge because so much was hidden from view. He waited for the men to go off duty and followed them here and there. They did not mind answering his questions on their way to the canteen, or even to the lavatory. This was how he had learned of many things that went on behind the scenes. Books and magazines told him plenty more. And the rest he imagined for himself. The railway system was like the insides of a gigantic clock, every wheel, lever, shaft, tooth, drum, spring, gear and weight playing its part with perfect precision.

His father had wanted him to become a doctor, but all Pulok ever wanted was to be an officer in the railways. The examination was tough and the competition formidable. But he breezed right through, then excelled in the training course, and caught the first available train to Pipli. So far, he'd had no problem at all. Yet, at times, he felt like he was being watched, as though he was somehow expected to fail. He knew, for instance, that at the end of his shift, his records were scrutinised with more than necessary care. This, he decided, was perfectly fair. All new officers needed guidance from their seniors.

'Shall I go then, babu?'

'Go.' Then he thought for a moment and motioned to the clerk to stay. 'Have you heard anything about me?'

Ramaswami looked puzzled, although he probably knew exactly what Pulok meant.

'You know,' he explained, sucking on his cigarette, 'sometimes people talk about others, man to man.'

Ramaswami pondered the question and shook his head from side to side.

'No? Nothing at all?'

Reluctant to disappoint the new assistant stationmaster, Ramaswami informed him that the sahibs had a different name for him.

'Really? What?'

'Chuckerbutty.'

'Chuckerbutty?'

'Yes, babu. Now I go.'

It struck Pulok that both the union representative

and the chief trains clerk addressed him as babu rather than sahib. Sahib was the master, babu a mere aide. He supposed he should not blame them for this mistake. Pipli was a small station and he was its very first brown sahib – the rest were Anglo Indian. Britishers held all the top posts in the railway department and Anglo Indians filled the middle levels. It was only recently that Indians had been appointed to anything but the lowest ranks. It would take a while for people to get used to it.

'Chuckerbutty,' he murmured to himself. It sounded strange to his ears. But many other sahibs had strange nicknames. The men often referred to stationmaster Peter Lazarus as Pete, though never to his face. Edward Menasse, the yardmaster, was called Ted. And cabin man James Adams was Jim. Yes, they were most welcome to call him Chuckerbutty. It was, in fact, an honour. It meant that they considered him one of them.

By 3.48 p.m., Chuckerbutty had finished updating the station diary. There was no change in the yard position. He had made a note of various messages from the control office. Caution orders for drivers to go slow over the Kalindi bridge were ready for issue. He had twelve minutes to spare before his shift ended. Nothing more needed to be done that day.

It was a pity that Pipli railway junction saw such a modest amount of traffic. Mail trains went through the main line without stopping. One express halted for six and a half minutes. That was all. Chuckerbutty often missed the excitement of Howrah.

A passenger train connected villages south of Pipli via the branch line. It was a popular service as the rural region had few metalled roads. Travelling by bullock cart was always slow, and next to impossible during the monsoon. So farmers took their produce to the local market by train. Men, women, and even children ferried forest products that they collected for sale – bundles of fuelwood, grasses, herbs, wild fruits and flowers. In season, they traded lac and honey, gums and resins. Off season, they fanned out in search of work. Pilgrims boarded the train too. Fares had been hiked twice in the last two years, but even this had failed to keep the villagers off the tracks.

Commercially, however, he knew that the loop line was far more important as it served the coal mines at Giridih. The railways relied on coal to fire its steam engines. Besides, factories demanded an endless amount, and the railways earned a handsome revenue from transporting it for them. The only problem was that coal had been in short supply ever since the war began. The railways needed more and more, and so did the factories – many of them now producing military supplies as part of the war effort. Clearly, the future of the country depended heavily on capable officers such as himself.

The smart click of heels echoed in the deserted corridor. Chuckerbutty glanced up from his papers just in time to see a flash of yellow in the doorway. Pen poised in midair, he waited and watched. There was silence. Nobody walked past the open window.

Puzzled, he stood up and went around his desk. A strange sound reached his ears – a gasp followed by a groan. He quickened his step. The heavy-duty Avery scale for weighing parcels was placed against the wall outside his room. It was flanked by his door to the right and his window to the left. If the shutters were open, they blocked the scale from view and an unwary passerby could walk right into it. This had never happened before, but there was always a first time.

A woman in a yellow dress was standing on the Avery scale. She did not see him emerge from his room. The sun was directly behind her. As it dipped lower in the sky, her hair turned to gold. He had made no sound, yet she turned her head. Her eyes were the green of tender mangoes. For an instant, he was paralysed. Then he hastily ducked out of sight.

7
Kitty

On Sunday morning, her father dismantled the gramophone and spread its insides on the dining table. He would spend several hours putting it back together and consider the day well spent. She could not remember the last time he went with her to church. Nobody reproached him for this. If they had, he would have told them to mind their own business. So her entire religious instruction had taken place at school – and miraculously survived her heathen holidays at home.

At the far end of the table, the soundbox was placed delicately on a soft cloth. The turntable lay beside it, its rubber surface wiped clean. She ran a finger down the winding handle. The gleaming metal was cool to the touch, ending in a well-worn wooden knob. Having unscrewed the motor deck, he turned it over and blew at it gently. For a while, Kitty sat at the table and watched him lovingly grease cogs and oil bearings. Then she got bored and stretched out on the living-room sofa with an Agatha

Christie novel. The servants had left for the morning. It was perfectly peaceful. At other homes, neighbours would drop in for a cup of tea in the afternoon or a drink in the evening. That sort of thing did not happen in the Riddle home. People knew that her father was never one for small talk and generally preferred his own company to theirs. If they did come over, there had to be a very good reason. And they were always careful not to stay too long.

He did talk though, when he felt like it. These days, he felt like it fairly often. He would go on endlessly about the war. His latest complaint was about the number of locomotives, carriages and wagons that had been sent to the Middle East. Originally, this was supposed to have been a stopgap arrangement. But the war was still going on, and its demands were only going up, not down. All this, she already knew. Everyone did. There was nothing anyone could do about it. Except have faith in the Lord and keep their fingers crossed. When she told him this, he laughed. She was glad he found it funny.

'Just don't say things like that at work,' she warned.

'How does it matter what I say?'

'It doesn't,' she admitted, 'but don't.'

He gave her a wry sort of look. 'You think the others don't talk? Well, they do. The railways are having to move far more troops and military supplies across the country. And since rolling stock is limited, the detention time in yards is being cut to achieve quick turnaround. You know what that means?' He did not wait for her answer.

'Less time for maintenance, less time for repairs. Running staff work longer hours – twenty, even thirty hours at a stretch. And at a time when we need more hands here, hundreds of railwaymen are serving overseas.'

Kitty pointed out that this was their patriotic duty.

'It's all very well to wave the Union Jack,' he muttered, 'but our railways will go to the dogs at this rate.'

Life was tough. There was nothing anyone could do about it.

Ayah glided by soundlessly in search of her father. Kitty told her not to bother him. A good quarter of an hour later, she realised that Ayah was sitting on the floor outside the dining room. Lowering the book, she asked what she was doing there.

'Waiting,' Ayah said.

'He's busy now, I told you.'

'Can you—'

Kitty continued to read. 'No, I can't,' she said.

At the end of the chapter, Ayah was still waiting. She was quite capable of sitting there all day.

'Tell me, what is it?'

'It's about my son—'

Kitty folded the corner of the page she was at. Servants always took ages to narrate their problems. She knew Ayah had a son because her father had helped him find work on the railways a few years back. He must have got into some scrape or the other and expected to be bailed out. Knowing her father, he would never say no.

'What did he do?'

'He joined the army.'

'Really?' It had not occurred to her that natives were serving in the army. But of course they were. The British empire stretched halfway across the world. Naturally its subjects had to fight for it. It was as much their patriotic duty as anyone else's.

'When was that?'

Apparently, one day last summer, he went off in a truck to be weighed and measured, came home, packed a few things and left. That was the last Ayah had heard of him.

'Didn't he write?'

'He doesn't know how.'

Kitty was not surprised. The natives did not take the trouble to educate themselves the way all civilised people did. They simply did not know what was good for them. That was why they would always be dependent on their betters.

'My heart says he is well because the money keeps coming, six rupees every month. But if Sahib can find out where he is—'

Kitty sighed. There was no need to bother her father with every little thing. Especially when he had worries of his own. She asked Ayah for the particulars.

Ayah handed her a piece of paper. Slipping it between the pages of her book, Kitty told her to go away.

Her father was out for the night. Latif produced kebabs and Jimmy brought beer. Pat and Dan were somewhere in the garden. Their company had become tiresome. Now that the two were engaged, they had stopped pretending that anyone else mattered. They held hands when they walked and locked eyes when they talked. At parties, they huddled in a corner until the slow numbers were played. Then they glued themselves to each other even as their indulgent parents looked on. She wished she had not called them over.

Despite all his tomfoolery, Jimmy was a serious musician. From Bing Crosby to Frank Sinatra, he sang them all. But in a style that was all his own. It was hard to describe his voice. Sometimes it was sensual, smoky. Other times, it sparkled like pure silver.

His fingers teased the strings of his guitar. The song was one of Jonathan's favourites.

Kitty made a face. 'Play something else.'

Jimmy obliged instantly. 'Yes, ma'am. Better?'

'Much better.' The chirpy little number held no memories for her.

'You belong on the stage,' she remarked as he broke into a raunchy ballad. He was always in demand at social events, and he obviously loved to perform.

He put down the guitar and took a bow. 'That's the plan,' he said. 'All I need is a break.'

'That's not going to happen here, is it?'

Jimmy rolled his eyes. 'In Pipli? No chance. I'm hoping for a transfer to Moghalsarai or Patna.'

Both towns had big railway colonies – he was much more likely to get noticed there. Military cantonments were promising too. 'How about Lucknow or Cawnpore? They've tons of railway and army folks. That's where you should be.'

'No,' Jimmy corrected, 'I should be in Calcutta, it's where the top musicians perform. I'm going to make a name for myself on the music scene. Then it's goodbye to being a fitter on the East Indian Railway.'

When it was almost midnight, Kitty yawned and said she was off to bed. Jimmy leapt off the banister and yanked her to her feet. Too sleepy to protest, she let herself be dragged to where Dan's bike was parked in the driveway. Jimmy eased it off the stand, turned the key in the ignition, and told her to hop on. Wide awake now, she looked down doubtfully at her bare feet before she swung a leg over the pillion. He kicked it to life and let out the clutch. The bike lurched forward, narrowly missing Dan, who had suddenly emerged from behind a rose bush. The roar of the engine drowned his anguished cry as they shot out into the ghostly lane.

At the flick of a switch, the headlamp snapped on, lighting up frenzied insects in its powerful beam. In a matter of seconds, they were at the main gate. Jimmy idled the engine while the watchman fished out the keys. Then the gate creaked open and, with another lurch, they were off. Kitty wondered what her father would say. This was probably not what he had meant when he said she needed to get out of the house.

Once the railway colony vanished from the rear-view mirror, Jimmy loosened his grip on the throttle and settled into an easy cruise. Kitty let go of her skirt. It rode up her bare legs and flapped about excitedly. Flanked by trees on either side, the road stretched ahead like an endless ribbon, dipping and rising, but not bending. Trees gave way to shrubs and the wind gathered force. Her hair whipped about her face, forcing her to close her eyes. The smell of wood fire told her they were passing a roadside village. In an instant, it was gone, replaced by the whiff of damp earth. The wind died down and the road turned to gravel, crunching as the wheels passed over it.

Just when it seemed that the night belonged to them alone, the yellow beam of the headlamp picked up the silhouette of an antelope. They screeched to a halt no more than ten feet away. The blackbuck stood stock still, unblinking and unafraid. A minute passed before it stepped off the path and was swallowed by the darkness.

Kitty tipped back her head to wish upon a star. There were not many to begin with. Then more emerged, one by one, jostling for space in the jewelled sky.

8
Terrence

Terrence Riddle stood outside the stationmaster's office. He had been waiting for all of fifteen minutes. There was no sign of the man. Typical, he thought. He did not think much of Peter Lazarus. In his opinion he should never have been promoted. A man in his position was supposed to take charge, but Peter Lazarus did nothing of the sort. He faithfully reported every matter to the higher-ups at headquarters and simply went along with whatever they said. Instead of pulling together the work of the commercial, operating, engineering and accounts departments, Peter just let them hammer things out among themselves. So far, there had been no major botch-up, but no thanks to him.

Peter hurried up and waved Terrence inside. 'Trouble in the parcel office,' he wheezed. 'Gave them a piece of my mind.'

His desk was more of a mess than usual. Peter sat on papers for as long as he possibly could. The project proposal for completing the new railway line to Giridih, for example, had not left his table for months. Terrence saw it buried under the stack of files before him.

'Some good news at last,' Peter remarked genially.

Aware of no such thing, Terrence did not comment.

'Surely you know about Tobruk?'

Terrence did not.

'El Agheila? Libya? The Middle East, man, the Middle East. What world do you live in, Riddle?' Peter cleared a portion of his table by transferring various files to the floor. Using his pen stand, inkpot, call bell and a glass half-filled with water, he proceeded to construct a map of North Africa.

Apparently Tobruk was a harbour near the Egyptian border. The Western Desert Force had taken a coastal city by the name of El Agheila from the Italians in early 1941. Rommel's Afrika Korps retook it not long after, and pushed the Allied forces back to Tobruk. The good news was that the British Eighth Army had finally managed to relieve the siege of Tobruk, and forced Rommel to withdraw to El Agheila.

'Our very first victory over German ground forces,' Peter explained, in case Terrence had overlooked this important point.

He had. Terrence was a courteous man. Courtesy demanded that he allow the stationmaster to elaborate on the strategic aspects of the victory. Once that was done, he cleared his throat.

'Sir, about that new line to Giridih—'

'Torpedoed, I'm afraid, Riddle, torpedoed.'

The stationmaster was restoring his desk to its previous state of disorder when the glass of water tipped over. He jabbed repeatedly at the call bell that was his Gulf of Sidra. As Terrence stood up to rescue a pile of reports, a peon rushed in, mopped the table, refilled the glass and covered it with a saucer.

The interruption shifted Peter's attention to a different theatre of war. 'The Pacific could prove to be tricky, to say the least. So many colonies, so many players – Britain, France, America, Holland. I hear even Portugal has an island out there. Fancy that.'

Terrence was not surprised at the fate of his cursed proposal. In all likelihood, the decision had been taken weeks ago, but nobody had bothered to inform him.

'The Japs have managed to take Hong Kong, Manila and Kuala Lumpur. But I can't say they're much of a fighting force. They could never have got this far if we had been fighting on one front instead of on two. And if the Yanks hadn't taken so bloody long to get into the war.'

It was quite possible that he was being kept in the dark about other matters as well.

'Now,' Peter mused, 'it all depends on which way Malaya goes. My guess is that once reinforcements arrive, our boys will thrash the Japs. As for Singapore, they'll never take it. Out of the question. Ultimately, it's all about leadership. And there's no better man than Archibald Wavell. The Yanks may have Douglas MacArthur and the like, but they're not a patch on our Archie.'

'What if they do?' asked Terrence, against his better judgement.

'Do what?'

'What if they do take Singapore?'

'They won't.' Peter Lazarus tapped the newspaper on his desk. 'I've been following the news, whatever little there is of it. The reports are obviously censored. Good news is padded up, bad news is watered down. You have to read between the lines to figure out what's going on. Take it from me, they won't.'

He rummaged in a drawer and waved a document at Terrence. 'That reminds me, the quarterly report is ready.' He turned a few pages and held it up. 'See this – charts and graphs, and in colour too. This new ASM is smart for a native. He has a funny way of talking, but he writes much better than Dobbs. What was it you wanted to see me about?'

'You asked me to see you, sir,' Terrence reminded him.

'Yes, of course, Riddle. It's about the branch line. HQ wants it dismantled.'

It was foolish for Terrence to be furious, yet furious he was.

The new line to Giridih had been 'torpedoed' because it did not matter. He should have seen it coming. The war effort had first claim on all resources. Railway works that were not of 'vital importance' had been on hold ever since the war began. Every government department had a tight budget during war-time, but the squeeze on the railways was not merely about funds. After all, its revenue had shot up spectacularly over the last two years. The squeeze was mostly over equipment.

Although the railway had come to India nearly a century ago, none of its essential components were manufactured within the country. They were imported instead, from countries that now happened to be at war, and shipped through channels that were no longer seen as safe. He knew very well that they were stretched for stocks. He also knew that the new line to Giridih could wait. But to dismantle an existing line and despatch it to the front was nothing short of absurd.

The branch line mattered. Every line mattered to the men who built it. All 62 miles of track and four wayside stations of the branch line mattered to him. Surveyed as early as 1893, it was supposed to link two grand enterprises one day – the East Indian Railway and the Great Indian Peninsular Railway. The route ran through the estate of a two-bit maharajah, who had refused permission to cut through his land. The East Indian Railway had sent its most persuasive officers to reason with him, but he simply would not budge. After he died, his eldest son was only too happy to be paid off, and construction began in 1919. Terrence had joined as an apprentice that year.

The construction camp was in a village called Satpuri. It had an open riverbank and plenty of fresh water. Plus, the headman had agreed to provide labourers at less than the going rate. Terrence remembered being surprised at how little they were paid. Tribals in those parts were gullible then.

It so happened that other outsiders were also in Satori at the time. A group of missionaries from Ranchi had pitched their tents not far from where the station was to be located. As he would later discover, their purpose was entirely different. So too were their dealings with the locals.

The plateau was flat for the most part and the jungle thick, virtually impenetrable. Where the soil broke cover, it was shallow and easily worked. But the bedrock was friable and in need of reinforcement.

Work progressed without a hitch. When the line from Belia to Dinapuri was completed a couple of weeks ahead of schedule, the officers decided to push on. This, it turned out, was not such a good idea.

The monsoon broke early and without any warning. Terrence was at the site of a bridge when the first rain fell. In a matter of seconds, the dry stream bed became a swirling mass of mud. The structure collapsed in the flash flood that followed. Five men were swept away along with the debris. One of them was an apprentice, just like himself. The camp closed down and the staff dispersed.

Three months later, they were back, keen to pick up the pace. Until a cholera outbreak brought work to a halt. The lethal bacteria bred in stagnant pools that stretched along the very embankments they had erected before the rains. The East Indian Railway evacuated its staff, leaving the missionaries to help the tribals deal with their sick and their dead.

The branch line was completed the following year, after villagers had first sacrificed a chicken to appease the spirits. This was not the Christian way, of course, but no railwayman saw fit to complain.

Peter's problem was that he could never say no. Any number of lines were termed as uneconomic. Any one of them could have been dismantled. When asked to destroy the branch line, he must have readily agreed. The stationmaster might get full marks for geography, but he knew nothing at all of history.

9
Chuckerbutty

Balancing his bucket and soap in one hand, Chuckerbutty hitched up the towel around his waist with the other. Usually he got to bathe first on account of seniority, but today a lampman stepped into the shared bathroom before him. Word had got around that the assistant stationmaster had not supported the case of the drunken khalasi. Chuckerbutty had known that the lower staff would be angry, but he had not expected them to show it in this way. Putting down the bucket, he let the towel slip, revealing the long underpants stitched by his mother. He dressed swiftly and flicked away imaginary specks of dust from his uniform. A pocket-sized mirror hung on the wall. He stepped back to get a good look at himself, then slicked down his hair with a dash of oil and combed it flat.

His window gave him an excellent view of the railway colony. The barracks were located at some distance from it, and his two-room quarters were on the second floor.

The main entrance to the colony was at the north-west boundary, while a smaller gate at the north-east end opened into the railway station. Four parallel lanes ran down its length, skirting a large quadrangle in the west. This was where the railway institute was located. The size of four bungalows put together, it was surrounded by a high hedge on all sides. A fishpond, a badminton court and a hockey field completed the square. A low fence served as the southern boundary of the colony, with a narrow gap for access to the barracks. There was no latch on the bamboo gate, but nobody ever opened it.

He enjoyed looking out at the whitewashed bungalows with their red-tiled roofs and green lawns, wondering what they were like inside. Sometimes he followed a figure down a lane, trying to guess who it might be and where it might go.

Right through the Christmas week, there was a steady flow of figures from one house to another, and to and from the institute. A lot of preparation must have gone into the festivities. Late one afternoon, he saw adults and children climb into sacks and hop across the hockey field. It was a type of race. Many of them toppled over and did not reach the finishing line. Other outdoor events were too far away for him to follow. On Christmas Eve, all the children were herded into the institute and a fat man in a red suit drew up in a tonga. It was Santa Claus. He had seen his picture in the imported magazines kept in the office library. At midnight, the church bell woke him up, and for a moment he mistook it for the fire alarm.

He was halfway into his trousers when he realised his mistake. It was difficult to go back to sleep after that. But there was no mistaking the music on New Year's eve. Propelled by loudspeakers, it entered his room and set the window panes abuzz. As he gazed out at the lights shimmering in the night mist, a desperate longing took hold of him. For what or for whom, he did not know.

Chuckerbutty was eager to learn as much as he could. Every week, he visited the library without fail. Many of the books there had never been issued before. These days, he was reading the reports of the railway board, taking precise notes as he went along. Now and then, he stopped to admire the way a complex issue was explained, the manner in which a table of statistics was analysed. This was what made the railways what they were – meticulous attention given to the minutest detail.

Some of these details took him by surprise. For instance, that miscreants cut telegraph lines running alongside railway tracks to pilfer copper wire. And that vandalism by the travelling public was rampant. Apparently light bulbs, fans and switch fittings were often stripped within a week of being put up. He also found out that hundreds of thousands of passengers travelled without tickets each year. He found it very puzzling that fines and imprisonment did not seem to have any effect at all. Perhaps the civil disobedience movement was turning ordinary people into petty criminals.

His hunch was confirmed when he studied the chapter on accidents. The railways were designed by foreign experts and managed by first-class officers. They should have been as safe in India as they were in England. Yet, a shocking number of people were injured, even killed, in sundry incidents. Last year alone, there were over four thousand cases of derailment. Although official inquiries had pointed to various technical lapses, he was sure that the real reason behind them was sabotage. Still, he could not see how causing death and destruction helped revolutionaries to achieve their goal.

Chuckerbutty put down his pen and gave the matter some thought. Then he resumed taking notes in his small but legible handwriting, the words spaced a finger's width apart. He drew a fresh sheet of paper and reached into the bottom drawer for an inkpot. Engrossed in wiping his inky fingers on a rag that he kept for this very purpose, he paid no attention to the knock on the door. It was only when it was repeated that he looked up to see who was there. Before he could say a word, she was standing five feet away. It was the woman with tender green mango eyes – only now they seemed to be blue. The next few minutes were a blur. She sat down at some point, but he could not later recall when or how this happened.

When he found his voice, Chuckerbutty asked if she would have tea. She refused politely. As was the custom, he asked her again. Again she refused. This, too, was the Indian custom. He was impressed that she should know. He rang the bell and instructed the peon to bring two cups of tea. The peon returned at top speed, but lingered over the decision on where best to place them. Chuckerbutty did not know what to do next. He took a quick sip and scalded his tongue. Luckily the woman decided to introduce herself just then.

'Pleased to meet you, Mrs Riddle—'

'It's Miss,' she corrected. 'Terrence Riddle is my father.'

Chuckerbutty hurriedly apologised. It was an understandable mistake, anyone could have made it. Miss Riddle was extremely charming, not at all like the forbidding assistant engineer. He hoped she had not come to talk about the Avery scale outside his room. That was not under his charge.

Much to his relief, Miss Riddle asked for his help in an entirely unrelated matter – finding out where her ayah's sepoy son was serving. Chuckerbutty was moved. What a noble sentiment. What a thoughtful gesture. He declared that he would be very happy to help. Miss Riddle had come to the right person, for he was in charge of matters pertaining to local employees. He had many close friends in the defence secretariat and would get in touch with them at once.

Miss Riddle took out a piece of paper from her purse. He recognised it immediately – such leaflets were distributed by recruitment agents to convince men to join the army. He had once met an agent who was on his way to a village fair to round up volunteers. These days, the military was having a lot of trouble finding recruits from the martial races of the North-West Frontier Province,

Punjab and Rajputana. That was why it had decided to look in other places, including Bengal and Bihar.

'His particulars are on the back.' She placed the leaflet on his desk.

He smoothed the creases in the paper and copied out the information with elaborate care.

'What exactly does it say on the other side?'

Chuckerbutty cleared his throat a couple of times. 'India springs to action,' he translated in what he hoped was a cultured voice, 'and stands side by side with Britain, America, Russia and China. Together our brave soldiers will trample underfoot the tyranny of Germany and Japan. Join them! Now!'

'This is a tiger,' he said, pointing to the snarling creature whose paws were planted firmly on the flags of Germany and Japan. Flags of the four Allied nations unfurled in the background.

'Yes, I can see that,' she said. 'I suppose it stands for India.'

Chuckerbutty agreed. Although its proper name was 'Bengal Tiger', he told her that the animal was found in other parts of the country as well. He handed the leaflet back to her. As she put it in her purse, he wished he could think of something intelligent to add.

Miss Riddle stood up, thanked him and left. It was some time before he noticed that she had not touched her tea.

That evening, Chuckerbutty sat cross-legged on his charpoy, placed a pillow on his lap and opened a file. It held the letters he had received in the three months he had been in Pipli. His sister Tuk-tuk kept him up to date with everything that happened at home. Her letters were full of complaints about their mother. These were countered by their mother with her own version of events. Her large handwriting filled all the available space, crawling up the margin on the left and down on the right. His friend Debu wrote that ever since he had cleared the entrance examination for the provincial civil services, he was flooded with offers of marriage. Chuckerbutty laughed to himself. Debu had been in love with the girl next door for years, but did not dare tell his parents.

The only postcard was from Sajal. He had been close to finishing his masterpiece when he ran out of art material. Chuckerbutty had quickly sent him a postal order for fifteen rupees. It was a large sum, but he could afford it.

Goku had taken over his father's cloth mill. He was minting money thanks to back-to-back orders from the war department. Manas was still flitting from one job to another. A bout of pneumonia had forced Jagat to give up smoking.

The most recent letter was from his father. It had arrived from Mandalay that very day. His father worked for the Irrawaddy Flotilla Company. This very fine firm transported passengers and goods on Burma's inland waterways. Its head office was in Glasgow and it owned the largest private fleet in the world. His father had joined at a time when Burma was still a province of British India. When it became a separate colony in 1937, relatives had advised him to leave. There was tension because the locals were accusing Indians of taking away their jobs. But he insisted on staying, and he never regretted it. Even today, a big section of the 10,000-strong workforce was from India.

His father visited the family in Calcutta every other month and wrote home every week without fail. His letters were long and eloquent, full of stories about fascinating people and places. To these he added his own thoughts – sometimes serious, sometimes playful, always wise. In his latest letter, he described his early days in the company – how difficult it was to fit in, how lonely the first few months were. How, every Friday night, he fought the urge to pack his bags and return home. Yet, every Monday morning saw him hard at work again. Six months passed before he felt that he belonged.

Chuckerbutty closed the file and put it back in the attaché case under his bed. His father was always so positive, so sure of himself. It was difficult to picture him as a lost and lonesome young man. Luckily he did not have to experience what his father had been through. He had always known that he belonged. One day, everyone else would know it too.

10
Terrence

'In Alcester lives a bonny lass, I think they call her Nancy;
Says she, a trip upon the line greatly would please my fancy.
I'll ride by steam and work by steam, by steam I'll on be hurried.
And when I can a husband find, by steam I will be married.'

Unable to remember the next verse, Terrence stopped humming. It was something to do with pigs and geese. Songs handed down the generations were still popular with railwaymen. This one was about the opening of a new line. Arches of flowers were erected along the route, cannons were fired, church bells rang, and thousands turned up to cheer. All this had actually happened – in a different time, a different place. Things were different now. New lines were abandoned midway and old ones were dismantled.

Terence smiled to himself and carried on to the chorus.

'Rifum tifum, mirth and fun;
don't you wonder how it's done?
Carriages without horses run—'

Age was catching up with him. His hair was still dark, but he often spied a hint of silver in his stubble while shaving.

As a young chap, he had found the first four months of his training deadly dull. He was confined to the Lillooah carriage and wagon workshop under a bully of a foreman who kept his nose glued to the grindstone. It was hardly an improvement over the life he had escaped in Madras, which was where he grew up. His father had started out as a salesman at a famous bookstore called Higginbotham's, and later became a copy editor in its publishing department. Terrence had no intention of ending up like him. When a distant uncle promised him a thrilling future in the railways, he did not wait to be asked twice. During those early months, he often wished that he had. But there was no question of going back home – not after the things his father had said when they parted. He was well and truly stuck in the dusty industrial town.

Luckily he did not have to sweat it out in Lillooah for very long. Out of the blue, he was sent to work on the

Pipli–Satori line. Either he had done something right, or his boss was fed up with him. Probably the latter. The work in the field was hard and the living conditions could only be described as primitive. But he was a fast learner. And every day was a new adventure. Construction was well into its second month when he chanced upon the missionaries' camp site.

The Mission was based in Ranchi town, roughly 80 miles due west. It ran an orphanage, a dispensary, and a residential high school for the natives. Over the years, it had opened a large number of primary schools in the surrounding villages and promising pupils – girls as well as boys – were encouraged to continue their schooling in Ranchi. The education they received was said to be better than that provided by the thinly attended government schools in the area. As word spread, more and more people in remote villages expressed a desire to educate their children. Satori was one such village.

A small group of missionaries was in Satori to set up a primary school. Eventually they would return to Ranchi, leaving trained locals to keep it going. Their camp was located in a clearing on the outskirts of the village – it was hard to miss. One evening, Terrence had followed two boys there. They were carrying a big kettledrum between them. He watched from a distance as they set it down and an older man strapped it on. It reached well below his knees. With a pair of drumsticks, he beat a rhythm that slowly picked up pace as well as force. Within minutes, the clearing was full. Men, women and children showed up out of nowhere and seated themselves on the ground. Terrence did not linger that day. But he did go back again – and again.

Initially he was reluctant to intrude, but the missionaries were a friendly lot. As the days went by, he found himself spending much of his free time with them. Theirs was a curious world, peopled by men and women of different nationalities. They lived just as the natives did, in the same kind of huts, eating the same kind of food. They even spoke the local dialect. At first he thought they were speaking Hindi – a language he barely knew at the time. Later, he realised it was quite different. It had surprised him once, to see a white man engaged in lively conversation with a half-clad woman, a baby strapped to her bare brown back. It was even more surprising to see her turn around for him to pet the child.

Some weeks later, the missionaries left. When there was a lull in work on the line, Terrence decided to make a trip to Ranchi. He went by road – the town was not yet on the railway map – travelling through the most beautiful countryside he had ever seen. Rugged ridges gave rise to sparkling waterfalls, and verdant woods clothed the rolling hills. Only occasionally was the scenery interrupted by a cluster of huts, for the region was only sparsely inhabited.

It was April. His friends at the Mission were expecting him during the week following Easter. He had planned to stay no more than a day. But that was before he met Annie.

'When the line is finished at both ends,
you may send your cocks and hens,
your ducks and turkeys, pigs and geese,
to any part wherever you please.'

He knew it would come back to him eventually.

Kitty popped into his office unexpectedly. When she was little, she used to come every evening and pry him loose from his chair, which she then promptly occupied. Her chin would just about clear the desk and her arms barely reached the pen stand. Busying herself with a paper and pencil, she would scribble away importantly, issuing stern instructions that he was supposed to follow. Afterwards, they walked home together, hand in hand. Every now and then, she tugged free to race ahead, hollering at him to catch up. He did so in a few easy strides, carrying her piggy-back till she wriggled to be set down again.

Everyone had warned him that it was not going to be easy bringing up a child alone. They were wrong. He managed just fine. He had no intention of asking some female relation to move in. In any case, he was no longer in touch with his family. An ayah was good enough, if not better. In the early years, his bosses were decent and posted him where the workload was light and travelling minimal. Kitty was perfectly happy, and so was he. Sending her off to boarding school was the hardest thing he had ever done.

He had left her at St Anne's and taken a room in

a railway guesthouse, to be able to check on her every day. After the first week, the principal told him that Kitty would settle in faster if he visited less often. So, on alternate days, he forced himself to watch from afar as she lined up for the assembly or ran about in the playground. When he returned from Darjeeling, the house felt terribly empty. But there was something of hers in every room – a ribbon, a doll, a little shoe. He ordered the servants not to touch a thing.

When she came home for the holidays, it was to a different railway colony, a different house, a different ayah. Although he would be transferred from place to place over the years, she remained firmly anchored at St Anne's.

'I'm thinking of going to Cal for a few days,' Kitty said. She perched herself on the arm of his chair and plucked at his sleeve.

The change would do her a lot of good. As far as he could tell, she was already less glum than before. He just hoped that Jimmy Mascarenhas had nothing to do with it. 'Any particular reason?'

'No, not really. I thought I'd have a look at some secretarial courses there. I think I'd make a good secretary. I'm very organised.'

The idea was totally ridiculous. When Kitty decided to take up teaching, he had approved. It was a noble profession. No matter what became of the present government, there would always be a demand for schoolteachers. Her future was secure – unlike his. It was a pity that she could not continue at St Anne's. Still, there were other good schools. Her qualifications were excellent and Sister Veronica would surely give her a decent reference. He forced himself not to react.

'Good idea,' he said, struggling with a drawer that was jammed.

'The new Alfred Hitchcock's showing at Metro next week. It's got Cary Grant and Joan Fontaine. I like Joan Fontaine. She was in *Rebecca* too. I might go.'

It was best to let her figure things out for herself. Sooner or later, she would. 'You can stay with the Conways.'

'Actually, I was thinking of the Byrds.'

Terrence nodded. 'Either should be fine.'

'Jimmy's going too,' she announced. 'They've asked him to sing at an official reception at the Howrah Railway Institute.'

'Really? I doubt he'll get leave of absence for that sort of thing.'

'Don't worry, leave isn't a problem. The stationmaster was the one who recommended him.'

Terrence swore as the drawer closed on his thumb.

An agitated peon came running after them as they made their way down the corridor. A gentleman had been detained for travelling without a ticket in a third-class coach of the express, and he claimed to be a friend of Terrence Riddle.

They headed around to the platform where the ticket examiner was waiting. Next to him stood a man in a shabby grey coat. He had his hands in his pockets and his back was to them. Even before he turned around, Terrence knew who he was.

11
Ayah

Latif strolled by, gently swinging a headless chicken by its feet. 'She's looking for you,' he said, waving a knife in the direction of the house.

Ayah nodded. She had almost finished polishing Sahib's boots. He was leaving early in the morning again. His uniform was not yet back from the dhobi. If it did not arrive by dinner time, she would go and fetch it herself. Raising a boot to the level of her face, she bared her teeth. Their reflection twinkled back at her. Satisfied, she gathered up the brushes and polish and swept the floor of the back verandah. After placing the boots in Sahib's room, she washed her hands and dried them on her sari. It was three days since she had spoken to Miss Kitty about her son. The piece of paper was all she had of him, she should never have parted with it. By now, it could be anywhere. Miss Kitty was always losing things. She needed help finding her own nose.

The girl was stretched out on the sofa as though she

had done a great deal of work that day. When she saw Ayah, she sat up, felt around in her skirt pocket, and took out the piece of paper that Ayah had given her. Ayah took it without saying anything. It was folded many times and one of its corners was dog-eared. What could she say? It was her own fault. She knew what Miss Kitty was like. She turned to go.

'I talked to the assistant stationmaster. He promised to help.'

Miss Kitty was talking nicely for a change. Ayah felt sorry for doubting her. She was not so useless after all.

'It'll take a few days to find out where your son is. You must be very proud of him.'

'Why?' Ayah asked.

'Because,' Miss Kitty explained, 'he is fighting for a just cause, to defeat evil forces. That's what this war is about.'

That was what all wars were about. People always thought the other side was evil.

'That's why so many countries are on England's side.'

'That's between them. This is not our war.'

'But it is,' Miss Kitty insisted. 'It's everyone's war. It's your war too. Can you imagine what will happen if we lose?'

Ayah thought this over. She did not see how it would change anything for her. 'He joined the army because he was hungry. Why should I be proud of that?'

After two failed harvests, they had mortgaged their land in Mitali and her husband had left for the coal mines. He sent money every other month and visited once a year. After a few years, the money stopped coming, and so did he. The moneylender took away their land. She had come to the railway colony then, to find a job looking after other people's children. Her own child was very young, but he did not give her any trouble at all.

Sahib had got her son a job as a casual labourer when he was old enough. The work was not regular. Sometimes he worked for ten days and sat idle for twenty. But when the new railway line started to be built, he worked every single day. He was not like the other boys. He gave her all the money he earned, not keeping any for himself. Bit by bit, they saved enough to pay off most of their debt. That was before the war came.

After the war came, the price of rice climbed higher and higher. They still managed to eat and they still managed to save, but not as much as before. Even though they ate less, their debt grew bigger. And then, all of sudden, work on the new railway line was halted. Some men from the nearby villages left for Giridih, others for Raneegunge. But she would not let the coal mines swallow him up. She told him to wait.

Others waited, but Ayah's son didn't. Now, finally, there was work for them on the railways again. Not to build the new line, but to take apart the old one. If only he had waited. Instead, he had gone away to fight someone else's war. What was there to be proud of? Nothing. Nothing at all.

Latif was very happy that there was a guest to feed. He always used to complain that Sahib did not invite people over. Now he made a special meal three times a day. The guest did not eat much, but he praised the food a lot. He was a different kind of sahib. Sometimes he came to the kitchen to watch Latif cook. He was a big man and she had to make herself small to go past him. He even offered to help Latif peel potatoes. He said he had a lot of practice. She saw his hands. They were rough, like hers, but his fingers were long and slender. Latif refused to give him a knife, though he let him stir a pot on the stove, just to be polite.

After Sahib left for work, the guest picked up a newspaper and went to the garden. She fetched him a chair, but he did not want it. He spread the newspaper on the damp grass and sat on it. Once, he plucked a cucumber in the vegetable garden and ate it standing right there. He said it tasted better that way. Most of the day, he just sat in the verandah. He never stepped out of the front gate.

Sahib wanted dinner served early, so Latif asked her to help him in the kitchen. She liked that. He ordered her around and made her do everything twice, but she did not mind. He became very talkative when he was cooking, though he only talked about food. The chicken curry was ready, swimming in a thick gravy that smelt strongly of garlic. Latif pinched a floret of cauliflower to see if it was done, and took the skillet off the fire. Then he handed her a coconut and asked her to crack it open and grate it. The coconut kept slipping and she nearly grated her fingers more than once. Meanwhile, he swiftly chopped two onions and two red chillies and ground them with some sugar, salt and vinegar. As a finishing touch, he threw in a fistful of raisins.

'Sahib's favourite, he will finish it all, wait and see.'

'Isn't that too much chilli for him?' she asked, studying the fiery red mixture.

Latif laughed delightedly. 'Without chillies, there can be no Devil's Chutney. Some sahibs look like white people and talk like white people, but inside they are just like us. Don't be fooled. Here, give me that.'

He would know. He had been cooking for sahibs all his life, as had his father before him. Ayah watched as he poured hot water over the grated coconut and squeezed out the milk. In a generous dollop of ghee, he fried some cloves, cardamom, cinnamon sticks and turmeric, and added the soaked rice and coconut milk. While it bubbled away on the stove, he darted around the kitchen, tossing pots and pans into the sink and wiping down the counter with vigorous sweeping arcs. The look on his face was one of undiluted joy.

As he transferred the food into serving dishes, Ayah hurried off to the dining room. Sahib was already hovering there. There was no sign of Miss Kitty. She took out the crockery and cutlery from the sideboard and set the table. Sahib did not care where the knife and fork were placed, but Miss Kitty did. She walked in while Ayah was filling the glasses with water. She looked at the table and did not say anything. After checking that everything was in its right place, Ayah left to pick up Sahib's uniform.

The dhobi had emptied out his iron by the time she arrived, but the coals were still alive. Despite being reminded, he had forgotten to press Sahib's clothes. She stood over him as he swung the heavy iron, the muscles in his arm bulging as he glided it over the tunic. Sweat glistened on his forehead even though the night breeze was cold. After scolding him one last time, Ayah left with the folded uniform draped carefully over her arm.

The dining room was empty when she got back. She stayed on to help Latif clear up. Leftovers went into the dhoolie; its steel mesh sides and door would keep them cool. Insects could not get into the small cupboard because its legs were standing in tin cans filled with water. After Latif finished washing the dishes, they walked to the outhouse in silence, parting at the hand pump in the courtyard.

The warm water from deep under the ground ran over her tired feet, splashing the edge of her crumpled sari. Her door was unlocked – there was nothing for anyone to steal. Removing her sari, petticoat and blouse, she wrapped herself in a coarse cotton cloth that encased her from chest to shin. In the village, she could wear a pandhat at all times, but here it was considered indecent. Resting on three bricks in the corner of the room was a small earthen pot. Two days ago, she had boiled a handful of rice, topped it up with water and left it to ferment. She ate this straight from the vessel, with a bit of salt and green chillies on the side. There was enough left for one more day.

Picking up the short broom kept behind the door, she bent down and swept away the dust of the day. Only then did she roll out a fine bamboo mat, one that she had woven before her wedding. Now pleasantly drowsy, she loosened her pandhat and let the rough woollen blanket chafe her bare skin.

Hours later, or maybe it was minutes, she turned on her side and tucked an arm under her head. That was when she sensed she was not alone. She was a light sleeper. Normally she could hear a footfall at the far end of the courtyard. Weariness must have made her careless. Perhaps she had forgotten to latch the door. Perhaps it creaked open without her knowing. Perhaps he crossed the room and lay down beside her without making a sound. Only the heat of his body gave him away. That, and the sudden twisting of her heart.

Her fingers ran through his unruly curls, tugging at the tangles to tease them free. She trailed a hand lightly over his closed eyes, feeling their lashes whisper against her calloused palm. Her thumb found the curve of his lips, but before they could part, she drew away. She willed herself to wait. If he so much as breathed her name, she knew she would be lost. Still, he neither moved nor spoke. Then, just when she felt she could not wait any more, he covered her aching body with his own.

12
Terrence

As the tranquil notes of *Liebestraum* wafted over the crunch of gravel underfoot, Terrence wished he had left for home sooner. Frank was seated in the verandah, his eyes closed. He had rolled up his shirt sleeves at the elbow – they were short for him in any case, ending well above the wrist. The clothes he wore when he arrived had been washed and given for darning. The white dog lay curled up under his chair and thumped her tail as Terrence approached, but did not leave her post.

When he returned after a wash and a change of clothes, the second section was almost over. It was years since he had played Liszt's love songs and the jacket was coated with a fine layer of dust. The white dog slipped out, gave his hand a quick lick and settled down again, her head nestled between his slippered feet. The melody pirouetted, delicate as a feather twirling atop rapids before it sailed into a serene brook.

'A fine collection you have here.'

'Not as fine as the one you have,' Terrence pointed out. It was Frank who had introduced him to classical music.

'Had. I only managed to save a few medical books, everything else was seized by your government.' He stretched his long legs and crossed one over the other. Then he said, 'It's quite instructive to discover how little one needs to live – if you can call that a life. I suppose we missionaries were the lucky ones. We had little to begin with, so we didn't miss any of the material comforts – like the businessmen did, for example. But it was hell – so to speak – not knowing what had become of the church, the Mission, the fate of our local pastors, our congregation. When they picked me up, I had several patients, some of them seriously ill. I wonder what became of them. I had trained quite a few local nurses, but they couldn't have kept the dispensary going, not on their own.'

'What was it you people were accused of?'

'Being nationals of countries at war with Britain. Of course we were guilty. Just as guilty as the hundreds of Germans, Italians, Bulgarians, Hungarians and Finns rounded up between Iraq and Hong Kong. From Ranchi, they took us to Ahmednagar at first. The Hostile Aliens Internment Camp, Ahmednagar, British India – that was our postal address. Later, they brought us to Premnagar near Dehra Dun. That's where hostiles residing in India were interned.'

'Odd name that, don't you think? Premnagar, city of love.'

Frank laughed. 'The camp wasn't as bad as you might

imagine. It was bearable. After a while, you get used to being confined. My wing — there were seven of them, separated by double lines of barbed wire — was for Germans. There must have been about five hundred of us, forty to a barrack. We called it Camp Teutonicus. We could see the majestic Himalayas by day and the night lights of Mussoorie reminded us that we were not far from civilisation. We set up a canteen, played football, exchanged books, talked. There was so much talking that I came to crave a little solitude. Inmates started study groups — on theology, for instance. It kept the mind alive. There were quite a few doctors, not just in our wing, but others as well. We were kept fairly busy. Old and sick interns were in a separate wing. They were the real sufferers. I'm ashamed to say I looked forward to being escorted there, if only for an hour or two, just to step out through the barbed wire fence around our camp.'

'Did they—'

'Torture us? No, they didn't have to. We did that to ourselves.'

The curtain moved and Terrence saw that Kitty was listening through the living-room window. She had turned the music down. Even so, the dreamlike quality of the evening persisted.

Frank turned his head slightly as if to address the window. 'The worst part,' he continued, 'was knowing that we wouldn't be freed till the war was over. And none of us knew what was happening out there. We had no radio, no newspapers. Letters were heavily censored. The occasional visitor was permitted, but there was no question of a private conversation. We were watched, all the time.'

'Another round?'

'Not for me.'

Terrence picked up both glasses and went inside. Kitty pretended to read a magazine while he poured two drinks and returned to the verandah.

'So how did you get out?'

'One of the guards helped. I had treated him for – shall we say – an embarrassing medical condition that he did not want revealed to his superiors. It's a long and amusing story. I'll tell you some time if you like.'

Frank found most things amusing, or so it seemed. The white dog sat up and yawned.

'You never know what freedom is till it's taken away from you. When you lose your dignity and self-respect, your faith in justice, in humanity, and – most of all – when you lose hope, it makes you reckless. A reckless man can do almost anything.'

It was just like the old days, nothing had changed. Frank would talk and he would listen. If Annie was here, she would have argued. But she was long gone.

Although it was late, he was not the least bit tired. Frank did that to people, he stirred them up. When they first met in Ranchi, he had only been there for a year or so. Yet, he was full of ideas, none of which he kept to himself. He had a view on everything, from the mundane to the metaphysical. Much of what he said went over Terrence's head.

At the time of the cholera outbreak on the railway line, Frank was everywhere at once – attending to the sick and the dying, cleaning up the filth, the muck. It was not the easiest job for a young doctor, but he made it look as though it was. Later, Terrence would discover that it was Frank's idea to teach native midwives safer ways to deliver babies in the villages. He toured the countryside and studied traditional remedies and medicines. These he tried out for himself, and put into practice those that he found effective. His hands were just as busy as his mind. He was the one who first made splints from the stiff spine of a palm frond, and casts from a mixture of egg white and herbs.

It was Frank who introduced him to Annie. A teacher in the Mission High School, she was the only person permitted to rap Frank on the knuckles when his tongue ran away with him. He would subside with good humour, looking on indulgently as she punctured his grand notions and poked fun at his fine words. They made a handsome couple.

Their courtship lasted six turbulent months, through fleeting visits and countless letters. Annie did not want to leave the compound where she had grown up. She did not want to give up teaching. And she did not want to part from Frank. Eventually she did all three. Frank was his best man at their wedding.

Annie did not take to railway life. Everybody was nice to her. Sarah Atkins took her under her wing and showed her the ropes. She made plenty of friends. She went for parties and joined in the fun and games. Nobody commented on her unusually dark colouring – at least, not in her presence. Instead, they complimented her blue-green eyes and her way with children. All the same, she did not quite fit in. A railway wife ran a tight household – Annie let his bachelor establishment run as it always had. She tried her hand at knitting and embroidery, only to give up in exasperation. Books held her interest for a while. Then she grew tired of fictional characters and their make-believe worlds. That was when she began to write. She wrote to everyone she knew in Ranchi, but most of all, she wrote to Frank.

The railway colony was too small for her. On sunny days, they wheeled out their bicycles and rode into the countryside with a picnic basket that they would open on the bank of a stream or in a grassy meadow. Sometimes they shared boiled eggs and jam sandwiches with villagers who opened their hearth to them, eating off leaf-plates. But these outings were not nearly enough.

Every few months, she took off for Ranchi, returning with stories of all that was happening at the Mission. The following year, these excursions came to an end. Stray incidents had been reported from various towns after the Indian National Congress launched its non-cooperation movement. When an English gunner was assaulted in a local bazar, security in the railway colony was tightened.

It infuriated Annie to be identified with the ruling class, but she promised not to venture out alone. By the time the movement fizzled out and restrictions were relaxed, she was pregnant. With a child she would not live to see.

Closing his bedroom door, Terrence unlocked the small almirah by his bedside. It held a few books, a bundle of letters and a box of photographs. He picked up a leather-bound volume that was missing a spine. It fell open at a much thumbed page.

> She walks in beauty, like the night
> Of cloudless climes and starry skies;
> And all that's best of dark and bright
> Meet in her aspect and her eyes;

There was no need for him to read the rest. All three verses were engraved in his heart.

23
Kitty

When Kitty found out that they were harbouring a fugitive, she was aghast. Her father had said nothing of the sort at the station. It was only later – when the man went in for a bath – that he mentioned it. Having him over for dinner was bad enough, letting him stay with them was madness. Her father did not even know how long it was for, he said it would be rude to ask. Besides, Frank Hoffman was an old friend. He was glad he had dropped by, and he did not see how this was anyone else's business. That clearly included her.

But it was her business. How could he forget that there was a war on, a war in which Germany was the enemy? Where was his sense of loyalty? It was not like him to give way to sentiment. He was always so correct, so proper. Yet, he was hobnobbing with the man instead of handing him over to the authorities. If anybody found out, that would be it. For her father and for her. How on earth could he not see that?

The first thing she did was cancel the trip to Calcutta with Jimmy. Tiresome, but it could not be helped. There was no way she could leave her father alone with that man. She told Jimmy that a poor relation was visiting from Poona, a tradesman in the printing business. Although they barely knew him, blood was blood, so they had taken him in. If anyone asked, this was what she would say. But nobody asked. Telling Jimmy was as good as telling the whole colony. Once that was done, she avoided the man and glared at her father whenever she got the chance.

The only time she was forced to put up with them was at the dining table. She made no effort to join in the conversation, eating quickly and excusing herself. From her room, she could hear them talk. Endlessly. Every now and then, her father would laugh. She had not heard him laugh like that before. These days, he was in no hurry to get to work. And he was back home before dark. The two took over the front verandah and argued loudly about which record to play next. The man usually got his way. Her father did not ask her to join him outside like he used to. But the white dog was always welcomed.

The music found its way into her room, so did the smoke. It curled in through the keyhole and the gaps in the hinges of her closed door. Her father did not smoke, nor did he approve of people who did. The arrival of Frank Hoffman changed all that.

Kitty found the man insufferable. He acted like he knew her father in a way that she did not, could not. If they were such great friends, why had she never heard of him? He had no right to simply drop out of the sky and make himself at home. She had lots of friends, but they were not family. Family was different, it was special. She and her father were family and there was no room for anyone else. On top of that, the man acted like he knew her too. It showed in the way he looked at her, indulgently, as if he could read her thoughts. In his crooked smile, as if he found her amusing. He had no right to smile that way.

There was no getting away from him even when she left the house, as she did to wish Mrs Wentworth on her thirtieth birthday. Mrs Wentworth said that her mother lived in Poona and could Kitty please ask her uncle to carry a parcel for her. Kitty explained that her uncle used to live in Poona but had lost his job and was now moving to Delhi. Mrs Wentworth was disappointed, but insisted that she take some cake for him and her father. Since neither of them deserved any kindness, Kitty ate both slices on her way home.

Her father would still be at work. That meant the man was in the house, alone. She took as long a route as she could, stopping by the institute. They were showing *The Great Dictator* that day. She stood in the darkened room for a while. A number of children had showed up for it, thinking that it was a comedy. She slipped out and headed home. It was ridiculous to allow the man to chase her out of her own home. The living-room lights were on, but the verandah was dark. She reached for the switch before she noticed him sitting in the shadows.

'You startled me,' she said accusingly.

'I'm sorry, I didn't mean to.' He shielded his eyes from the bright light. 'Won't you sit down?'

Kitty did not see why she should. She crossed her arms and leaned against the banister.

'I suppose you want to see me gone.'

How perceptive of him, she thought.

'I know I shouldn't have come. It was not right to impose on Terrence—'

And on her.

'And on you.'

If he expected her to disagree, he was mistaken.

'You remind me of your mother. She was about your age when she left the Mission. How old are you – twenty-one? Twenty-two?'

It was rude to ask a lady her age. Surely he knew that.

'No,' he said after some thought, 'you must be nineteen.'

Kitty traced the contours of a knot in the smooth wood. What was the point of asking her if he knew the answer?

'Annie could never hide what she was thinking, it always showed on her face, in her eyes. You have her eyes – your father must have told you that.'

Her father did not talk about her mother. All he had told her was that she was an orphan, brought up by missionaries in Ranchi. That she taught in a school before they got married. And that she died soon after giving birth.

People talked such rot about Anglo Indian orphans. There were tales of tea planters who took local mistresses, of soldiers in the lower ranks who slept around, of well-bred girls seduced by native men. The offspring might end up in an orphanage like Dr Graham's Home in Kalimpong or St George's Home in Ooty.

'It didn't bother her,' the man said, interrupting her thoughts. 'Not knowing who her parents were, what they did, where they were from. The missionaries gave her a home, but she chose her family herself. Not everyone was admitted, she was very picky that way. So are you, I imagine.'

He was smiling that crooked smile again. Kitty pursed her lips.

'You were lucky if you got picked. I was one of the lucky ones.'

Kitty sighed and wondered if there was a point to his boring sermon.

'I plan to be on my way very soon. But I wanted to meet you first. It was one of the reasons I came.' He went to the guest room and returned with a booklet that he held out to her. She took it without comment. 'Annie was planning to start a school. The idea came to her during her confinement – I don't know why it took her so long. It was the obvious thing for her to do. She was a born teacher.'

It was a nice thought. But there were plenty of schools for railway children.

'None of the ayahs knew how to read or write. She wanted to start with them. Annie could be very persuasive. She said it would be easier to educate children if their mothers could read and write.'

A school for ayahs – how quaint.

'She asked me to send her primers from Ranchi. We used to print them at the Mission. I put a set together, but by the time I got around to sending it, it was too late. There were twenty of them, I managed to save just one. I thought you might like to have it.'

Kitty glanced at the primer in her hands. It was at least as old as she was. The edges were frayed, but it was otherwise intact. She had no idea what to do with it.

'You'll figure it out,' he said.

She looked up to see if he was smiling. He was not. He pushed back his badly cut hair with an unsteady hand. The fine lines on his face had deepened, making him look weary, even a little frail.

'So,' she said brightly, 'where will you go next?'

This time, his lips twitched. 'I have to lie low for a while, till the search is called off. Don't worry, I'm not staying. I know my way around. Plenty of people would be happy to have me.' His face was perfectly straight now. 'After that – I really don't know. The world is such a big place, isn't it? If you look hard enough, you can find beauty and meaning anywhere.'

The next morning, only two places were set for breakfast. The man was gone. She should have been delighted. Instead, she only felt confused.

14
Terrence

Terrence watched from a distance as labourers unloaded rails from a lorry. It was a slow process. Each length of rail was suspended in slings at four places, each sling shouldered by one man. The four men moved in tandem. A single misstep as they came down the ramp could result in damage to the rail, if not to a foot.

The first section of the branch line had been dismantled. The original plan was to store the material at a wayside station till the work in that particular section was complete. But the risk of theft was high and the station's watchmen would be no match for armed robbers. An additional contingent of railway police had been requested, but this would take time to materialise. Peter Lazarus could no longer fend off impatient officials at headquarters. So, as soon as a lorry-load of material was removed from the line, it was transported to the goods shed at Pipli. The lorries would ply right through the month and well into March.

When the dust cleared, Terrence made his way to the shed. Stanley McBride was smoking outside. He ground out the cigarette stub as Terrence approached. Of the three permanent way inspectors, he was easily the most accomplished. This came across not only in the way he worked, but also in the way his entire team worked. The men put in their very best, knowing that he would accept nothing less. It was no surprise that they looked up to him, for he always looked out for every one of them.

The two men walked over to the far end where the rails and sleepers were being sorted. Crates of fittings were stacked nearby. Fishplates, bolts, keys and dog-spikes were each packed separately. The material would be graded according to its condition. Certain items were re-usable in running lines, others in yards and sidings. Worn out rails would serve as posts or beams. Defective sleepers would be fashioned into keys or plugs, or else used for paving and scantling. The rest would end up as scrap. Each lot had to be accounted for and valued – a separate project in itself.

The grading of fittings was already under way. The men were working in three shifts to complete the task on schedule. A daub of white paint marked items for running lines, while yellow indicated those intended for non-running lines. Items for sundry uses as well as scrap were marked with red paint. The branch line had seen relatively light traffic, so the bulk of the fittings would be good enough for reuse in the running lines. The stationmaster would be happy to hear this.

A trolley piled high with damaged sleepers clanged towards them. Terrence and Stanley got out of the way and moved out to the goods yard. It was deserted but for a pair of mynas pecking about in the dirt. Terrence did not believe in small talk, so he came straight to the point. He said he needed Stan to cook the books.

Stanley did not blink, as though he received such instructions every day.

Having stated the purpose of their conversation, Terrence proceeded to explain. 'I've been getting complaints about the loop line, vibration is excessive at places – a number of places. Last week I saw this for myself, when I travelled the entire route in the brake van. The drivers are right.' He had no doubt that the massive increase in traffic of coal wagons had worn down rail joints at these locations, and on-site examination confirmed this. What was most disturbing was that the damage was recent– implying that further deterioration would be rapid.

'It's bound to get worse, fast. And,' he continued, 'as you well know, we're low on stocks of fittings.'

'We placed orders—'

'Three months ago, I know. But I believe other stations placed orders too, many of them well before us. I'm told that local production is way short of demand and imports are held up at sea.'

'In which case, I reckon we shouldn't expect to be supplied anytime soon.'

'That's right.'

A khalasi went by with a low salaam. Terrence waited till he was out of earshot.

'I've thought this over, and there's only one thing to do – hold back a decent batch of fittings coming off the branch line. Record them as scrap, and use them to repair the loop line.'

This time Stan did blink, but he was quick to catch on. 'So we show the defective fittings from the loop line as scrap from the branch line.'

'Exactly. Once you've made the switch, you'll have to reconcile the numbers in the books.'

Stanley pointed out that the books could not be kept open for long.

'True, which is why you need to hurry. Involve as few men as possible – I don't want word getting out.'

'But if it does? You know how chaps talk, especially after a couple of drinks.'

'Well, that's a risk. But the responsibility is mine – remember that – not yours, not theirs.'

Stanley reached into his pocket for a cigarette, but did not light it.

'Don't worry, it's a trifling quantity, it won't be missed. HQ will manage just fine.' They had to manage. Supplying the war was their top priority. His top priority was to make sure that the lines under his care were safe.

His plan made perfect sense in the larger scheme of things. A year ago, he would have been livid at the mere suggestion of such impropriety, even if only made in jest. As he strolled back to his office, Terrence was surprised at how easy it was to subvert the system.

They did not make railwaymen the way they used to. In a certain sense, the railways had much in common with the police, even the military. It was a uniformed service. There was a chain of command. Discipline was imperative. Deviation from norms had a cost – not merely in terms of time and money, but also in terms of human life. In his time, railwaymen were trained to follow orders, but they were also expected to apply their minds. They took calculated risks. They were bold, resourceful, ingenious.

The younger lot was different. They were willing to work hard, but reluctant to take the initiative. They preferred to be instructed rather than think for themselves. When the time came for them to make decisions, they would rely solely on precedent. But times were changing. New problems called for new solutions. This was where they were weak. To be fair, it was not entirely their fault. They lacked mentors who could help refine their skills, sharpen their instincts, develop their character. Seniors – himself included – no longer gave them as much time as they should. Instead, they were busy filing reports and filling proformas.

One day, the likes of Jimmy Mascarenhas would be running the railways. It was a sobering thought. Before he could digest it, the assistant stationmaster hurried past, his body bent awkwardly in a semi-bow. Chuckerbutty was rarely visible outside his office. He kept his head down and put in long hours. As he should, Terrence thought. It was his first posting and he needed to prove himself. Doing well in his early years would stand him in good stead later on. The chap was definitely bright and had already established his integrity. But someone ought to tell him to take some time off or he would burn out before too long. It was a pity that Peter Lazarus was his first boss – there was nothing to be learned from that quarter.

Terrence hailed the young man. Chuckerbutty stopped dead and turned around in slow motion.

'How are things?' Terrence asked.

Chuckerbutty started. 'Things are very fine, sir,' he said.

'That's good.' A pigeon waddled along the overhead ledge with its chest puffed out. 'Do you care for birds, by any chance?'

'Birds, sir?'

'Yes, birds.' He pointed upward.

'Birds are very fine, sir.'

'Very fine indeed. Have you heard of the Great Pied Hornbill?'

Chuckerbutty admitted that he had not.

'No? You may know it as the Great Indian Hornbill. You don't? Well, let me tell you, it's a fascinating bird – I've seen it a couple of times in these parts. Do you know how it nests?'

Chuckerbutty looked embarrassed. Terrence gave him a kindly smile. 'The couple builds a nest in the hollow of a tree trunk. The male seals the hole from outside, and the female seals it from inside. But they leave behind a slit – clever, don't you think?'

Chuckerbutty nodded.

'For a month or two, the female stays inside the hole

while the male brings food for her, and for the chicks, once they hatch. Now, if he were to die, the whole family would perish. But let's say he doesn't. The chicks grow up, break the seal and fly away. Fascinating, isn't it?'

'Yes, it is, sir.'

Terrence was pleased. 'When I was your age, I used to study birds. I could identify any bird in the area by hearing its call. It's an excellent hobby. You should try it some time.'

'Yes, sir, I will. Thank you, sir.'

'Do that. You will enjoy it. I'll send across a pair of binoculars tomorrow morning, I haven't used them in years.'

Chuckerbutty was speechless with gratitude. Terrence shook his lifeless hand and went on his way.

15
Ayah

Ayah looked down at the stain on her sari. She had tried to wash it out two hundred times, but it refused to go away. At first she would hide it among the folds of her sari and hope that nobody saw it. But now, she did not care if they did.

Two girls were sitting on either end of the see-saw. One was fat, the other was thin. When the fat one came down, she leaned back and left the thin one up in the air. She let her kick and scream for a while. As soon as the thin girl's feet touched the ground, she jumped off. The fat girl dropped like a stone. Clutching her bottom, she ran after the thin one. They chased each other around the monkey bars before heading for the fishpond hand in hand.

The grass was soft beneath her and a light breeze lifted the tendrils at the nape of her neck. Hugging her knees, she closed her eyes and let the February sun warm her upturned face. When she opened her eyes, the ayah from B-6 was coming through the trees carrying a large child in her arms.

'You should let him walk,' she advised Bela, 'it's good for him.'

'I know, but he gets tired, poor baby.' The boy patted her head happily as she pulled up his socks. 'Your sari is stained,' she observed, giving him a little push.

As soon as he was free, the boy set off as fast as his short legs could carry him. When he reached the bottom of the slope, he climbed back on all fours before hurtling down again. When he grew tired of this game, he put out his arms and turned round and round like a top. All of a sudden, he stopped and swayed on his feet. After taking a few wobbly steps forward, he sat down with a bump. For a moment, it seemed like he was about to cry. Then he changed his mind as a tuft of grass caught his eye. Reaching out with one chubby hand, he plucked a fistful of grass and stuffed it in his mouth. Bela rushed up and made him spit it out. The boy clambered to his feet and trotted off after a squirrel.

Bela sat down again and sighed. 'Shall I tell you what happened yesterday?'

'No,' Ayah said, knowing that Bela would tell her anyway.

'Yesterday, that Soni—'

'The carpenter's wife?'

'No, Birju's daughter, the older one. Yesterday, Soni left her house early in the morning and went to cut grass in the jungle. Her younger sister went with her, but she came back at noon. Soni went deeper into the jungle. By evening, she was not back. Birju took five men with him to look for her. They looked everywhere. They didn't find her. But you know what they found?'

'What?'

'They found Soni's sickle. Under a bahera tree. The shrubs around it were flattened. Can you imagine?'

Ayah shook her head.

'Birju has gone mad, poor man.'

The boy dragged a dead branch towards them. It was heavy, and he was panting with the effort. Bela started to get up, but Ayah caught her arm.

'She'll be back, she knows her way.'

'I know, that's what I said. But the world is such a wicked place, isn't it?'

The boy dropped the branch and made his way to a nearby bench. A crow swooped down over his head and cawed rudely. The boy did not stop. Holding on to the bench with one hand, he reached beneath it with the other. Soon he was back with a pebble that he placed carefully in Bela's lap. He went back and forth, each time returning with an offering – a leaf, a twig, a handful of earth.

'Now he's happy. For so many days, he was so sad.'

It was true – the world was a wicked place. But Soni was a clever girl. She knew how to look after herself. Nothing wicked would happen to her.

'He kept crying for his mother, but Memsahib couldn't go to him. She was too upset.'

Still thinking about Soni, Ayah asked her why.

Bela said that her memsahib's brother lived in a place where many bombs fell from planes in the sky. Some people ran away, some were left behind. Her memsahib did not know if the poor man was safe or not. Nobody knew what was happening there. All day long, she listened to the radio. She hardly ate anything, just biscuits or toast. At night, she kept getting up to check the door. Sometimes she fell asleep on the sofa. The cook would find her there when he came to serve tea in the morning. Finally a telegram had arrived, just after breakfast today. The brother was all right. Her memsahib was very happy, but she kept crying for a long time. Now she was sleeping. She had suffered so much, poor woman.

'Which place was it, do you know?'

Bela was not sure. But she thought it was somewhere in the east.

The boy came towards them, a feather clutched triumphantly in his little fist. He threw his arms around Bela's neck and she smothered him with kisses.

'Don't love him too much,' Ayah advised, 'it's not good for you.'

The platform was empty except for the fruit seller. Business was bad these days, but he still came without fail. She went up to him and asked how much for an apple. He shook his head and felt around in his basket. Then he handed her an apple with a brown hole in its side. She did not want to take it, but he insisted. He rearranged his basket and asked her the time.

She looked up at the station clock. It was eleven hours and forty minutes. Sahib had taught her how to tell the time. He said everyone should know this much. There was a big clock in the dining room. He had taken it down and showed her how to count the hours and the minutes. He even opened the back and explained what made the two hands move. In the beginning, she would stand in front of the clock and count slowly. But after a few days, she could tell the time while walking past the clock. Sahib said she was very clever. She wished this were true.

Some days, she opened the newspaper the way Sahib did, running her eyes from left to right, top to bottom. Some words were big, others were small. They told her nothing. One by one, she turned the pages and looked at the pictures. They were of important people who did important things. She did not know who they were or what they had done. When her arms grew heavy, she folded the newspaper neatly and put it back where it belonged.

If she knew how to read, she could find out why so many trains were going east without stopping. She asked many people, but nobody would tell her. Instead, they told her terrible things that she did not want to know. There were giant man-made fish that swam secretly under the sea, searching for ships to destroy. There were bombs hidden in the soil, like traps for wild animals. When a man stepped on one, it exploded, scattering his flesh far and wide. There were guns that fired a hundred bullets, one after the other. They sliced a man's body in half as though it was a potato. Some guns spat fire instead of bullets, others a poisonous gas. There were so many ways in which a soldier could die.

It was twelve hours and forty-five minutes. A train pulled in, but did not stop. It was going east, where bombs fell from planes in the sky. Soldiers were crowding around the doorways and leaning out of windows, tossing out banana peels and waving as they went by. Joking and laughing as if they were off to a fair. Maybe they did not know where they were going, maybe they did not care. Maybe it was better not to know, not to care.

When she saw a pomegranate tree for the first time, its branches were hidden by shiny leaves and showy red flowers. Her son had tried to climb it – he was small then – but the sharp spines made him jump down at once. Over the next few weeks, they had watched as the petals shrivelled up and the strange fruit took shape. It was hard and leathery to the touch and they had never seen anything like it. He split one open and admired the rows of glistening beads inside. Squirrels and birds came from all over the garden to nibble them. He nibbled too – though she warned him not to – and pried out a handful for her to nibble as well. Together they ate the lot, swallowing the syrupy juice and spitting out the hard seeds. That day, he wiped his hands on her sari. The crimson stain never went away. She hoped it never would.

When they came to B-15, he had planted a pomegranate seed outside their window. She told him that it might not sprout, but it did. He watered the seedling every day and built a bamboo fence around it. She told him that it might not survive, but it did. He manured it and kept it free of weeds. She told him that it might not grow, but it did. It grew bigger and bigger till it reached above their window and cast a shadow into their room. He propped up branches that sagged and snapped off those that were dead and brittle. She told him that it might not bear fruit. This time she was right. Sometimes all the love in the world was not enough.

16
Chuckerbutty

The onion pakoras were golden and crisp. Chuckerbutty munched on, licking the mustard oil that greased his fingertips. After retiring as a coolie, Krishna had set up a tea shop at the main crossing of Pipli town. The small thatched shack with four rickety tables was popular with locals and visitors alike. Before long, he added a wooden cabinet with a glass front to display his wares, as well as a radio to entertain his customers. Out of loyalty, he offered a generous discount to railway staff. Their help in getting kerosene in times of scarcity more than made good his loss.

All through that week, villagers camped on the platform, waiting for the arrival of the passenger train that would take them south. They were told that there was no longer such a train, but this they did not believe. Each time they heard a rumble in the distance, they gathered their luggage and stood at the edge of the platform, ready to leap on when the train stopped. When it did not stop, they sat down again. By the end of the day, the crowd trickled away. By the morning, a fresh lot arrived. They too would wait for the arrival of the passenger train that would take them south. They too were told that there was no longer such a train, and they did not believe it either.

Since the assistant stationmaster was supposed to deal with travellers' complaints, they were all directed to his office. The men rushed in, wives and children in tow, touching his desk, interrupting his work. Most of them were confused and anxious, unable to understand what had changed. Some were annoyed, even aggressive. One man offered him money, as though this would miraculously restore the train service. Eventually he put two railway constables on duty to shoo them away.

The men seated behind him ordered another round of tea. Krishna seemed to know them well, because he threw in extra milk without being asked. Judging from their talk, one was a local farmer and the other was some sort of trader from Ranchi. The farmer was saying that his daughter was getting married to a peon in the district telegraph office. He insisted that the trader must come for the wedding along with his family. The trader declared that he surely would.

'What's the going rate for a peon these days?'

'I can only say what I'm giving – four cows, a bicycle and a sewing machine.'

The trader remarked that he had got off cheaply. Privately, Chuckerbutty agreed.

'Cheaply? I had to take a hefty advance from the village grain merchant. My daughter is still sitting in my house and he's already hounding me for his money.'

'And what did you say?'

'I said to wait till the wedding is over. What else could I say? Then I'll sell my paddy and pay him back.'

The trader said he hoped the wedding was a long way off. 'Because, my friend, the price of rice is shooting up like anything. I won't be surprised if it soon doubles.'

'It is? Are you sure?'

'Would I say anything if I wasn't sure? Ask anyone in Ranchi if you don't believe me.' The trader sounded very confident. 'Postpone the wedding,' he urged his companion. 'Wait a few weeks before you sell your paddy. Then pay the merchant and buy as many sewing machines as you like.'

'I can't do that. It won't look good. What will people say? What reason can I give?'

'There are many good reasons to postpone a wedding. Say there's been a death in the family.'

For a while there was silence. Then the farmer spoke up. 'My maternal grandmother's brother-in-law's wife expired three days ago.'

The trader assured him that this would do. Having settled the matter, he then revealed that he was selling a new product these days. 'A medicine called Aspro. It's imported. Cold, fever, rheumatism, gout, malaria – it cures them all. I can't tell you how popular it is in the big cities, everyone is buying it. One anna for three tablets, or ten for thirty. Here – for you it's free. Try it and then tell me.'

Krishna tuned in to the Hindi broadcast of a popular German radio station. Its music programmes were lively and the reception was usually good. Although the station was banned because of the war, people still listened when they were sure they could not be reported.

Chuckerbutty wiped his hands on a scrap of newspaper and lit a cigarette. A group of women were walking by with bundles of firewood on their heads. They must have spent the day gathering it from the jungle beyond the outskirts of the town. They were hurrying along, for dusk would fall soon and the evening meal was yet to be prepared. But, as they came closer, their bare feet slowed to match the rhythm of the song on the radio.

There were about twenty of them, maybe twenty-five. Unlike city women, they did not wear blouses. Instead, their sarees were wrapped tightly around their bodies. The bouncing of their breasts was a beautiful sight. As they filed past, he leaned forward and stretched his neck as far as it would go. The song ended. The women disappeared from view. A long column of ash fell unbroken into his tea.

Chuckerbutty did not crave for the life he had left behind in Calcutta. He was very contented in Pipli. Only one thing was missing – the company of women. He missed his mother's quiet sense of humour. The flash of his sister's eyes when she was angry, which was often. Teasing the upstairs tenant's daughters. Gossiping with the old ladies down the lane and flirting with the younger ones. He missed the lure of a suggestive glance, the heat of a provocative touch. He had not known how much he missed these things, until the moment Miss Riddle walked out of his room.

After shooting off a telegram to his army friend in Calcutta, he had plunged into the files on his desk, clearing them at top speed. Miss Riddle would be back. This time he would be his normal self — witty and wise. They would engage in intelligent conversation. There were many important matters to discuss. He knew that she had a fine mind. Clearly she must be very well read. Perhaps she was familiar with the writings of Rabindranath Tagore, the only Indian to win the Nobel Prize. He wondered if she had read *Ghare Baire*. The English translation was called *The Home and Outside*, or maybe *The Home and the World* — he could not remember which. The hero of the novel was educated. He appreciated Western culture. He believed that women must step out of the home and experience the outside world, form their own opinions, make their own choices. He was rational, civilised. He was against aggression, even as a means to achieve the noblest of goals. If she read the novel, Miss Riddle would come to know that he too possessed those very qualities. He would gift her a copy if she did not have one already.

The arrival of the binoculars was timely. He had no idea that this simple instrument could be so educative.

Just a few sessions at his window taught him so much about Miss Riddle. In the early morning, she was rarely visible. At times she sat outside with a book, shifting her chair as the shade moved across the garden. On some days she wore a big hat to shield her face but let her naked arms and legs soak up the sun. She liked bold colours, especially red. Red was the colour of purity. One day, he saw her leaving her house in the yellow dress that she had worn when she stood on the Avery scale. Yellow suited her. He followed the yellow dress down the garden path, out of the gate, down the lane. Then he blinked, and it vanished. He searched the surrounding area, but there was no sign of it.

That day, it was difficult to concentrate on work. He got through his shift, returned to the barracks and went straight to his window. Miss Riddle was in her garden, lying on the grass. He was glad that she was back in the safety of her home. In the evenings, he always did a quick sweep of the railway colony. The entrance to the institute was lit well enough for him to see dim figures moving in and out. Even when the rest of Miss Riddle's house was dark, the verandah light was always on. On one occasion, he saw a couple fused together under a lamp post outside her gate. Miss Riddle would never stand on the road and embrace a man in full public view. She was not brought up to behave that way.

A small boy carrying a large stick was leading a herd of goats down the road. As he stopped to listen to the music, the goats scattered in all directions. One of them strutted into the tea-shack. Its horns were sharp and twisted, and a leafy twig dangled from its lips. The thatch shook as the goat scratched its head against the bamboo pole propping it up. The song ended. The boy moved on. So did the goats.

When the evening news bulletin began, Chuckerbutty stood up and reached for his wallet. He had kept the tonga waiting outside. The distance from the railway station to Pipli town was not that much, but it was not proper for an officer such as himself to be seen walking along the dusty road.

Static interrupted the broadcast. Krishna adjusted the frequency and increased the volume. German U-boats were apparently shelling oil refineries in the Caribbean Sea. Their aim was to cripple fuel supplies to English, French and American airplanes. And in Asia, Japan had won yet another 'glorious' victory in the Pacific. The flag of the rising sun now flew atop all the important buildings in Singapore. The fall of the island fortress was the 'most humiliating' defeat suffered by Britan in its 'entire military history'.

Chuckerbutty sat down again.

The news reader's voice continued. The two commanders-in-chief had signed the terms of surrender at the 'magnificent' Ford automobile assembly plant. Japanese reporters, photographers and newsreel cameramen were present in 'huge' numbers for the event. Among the 60,000 prisoners of war were 16,000 British, 14,000 Australian and 32,000 Indian soldiers.

General Toto had declared that all major British and American bases in East Asia were now in Japanese hands. However, he warned his people not to be 'too elated' over the taking of Singapore. For this, he said, was 'only the beginning'.

At this point, the farmer asked the trader if Singhapur was anywhere near Singhbhum, because that was where the groom's family was from. The trader laughed long and hard, thumping the table at regular intervals. The rest of the bulletin was inaudible.

Chuckerbutty tried to visualise the map of Asia. He knew that Singapore was south of Burma, but he could not place it precisely. Wondering exactly how far it was from Mandalay, he paid Krishna and left.

17
Ayah

Miss Kitty was in a bad mood. It started when the guest came to stay, but did not go away when he left. Even when Sahib talked to her kindly, she replied as if there was a stone in her mouth. She was mostly in her room with the door bolted. Or else she was out with her friends. There were three of them – the tall boy from C-2, the girl from C-9 and Master Jimmy. Master Jimmy was a nice boy, very friendly. All the servants in the colony liked him. He was good for Miss Kitty. Maybe he was too good for her.

Twenty-one days had passed since Miss Kitty promised to find out where her son was. Twenty-one days was a long time, long enough for a hen's egg to hatch. Ayah thought of reminding her on the tenth day, but did not want to irritate her. So she kept quiet. She hovered nearby so that she could go quickly if Miss Kitty called. She did call, two or three times, but only because she had lost something. These days she was losing many things, including her temper. The next time she called her, it was about the books.

'Look,' she said angrily, 'just look at this. It's upside down.' She handed the book to her and picked up another from the shelf. 'So is this one,' she said, 'and this one and this one.'

'I always arrange them like this.'

'Well, you always arrange them wrong. Can't you see?' She went on taking out books and adding them to the pile in Ayah's arms. 'This is up, this is down. Can't you tell the difference?'

Her voice was very loud. Sahib came out from the bathroom in a towel to see what had happened. Miss Kitty showed him the books. They were talking in very fast English, so she went away.

Sahib called her in the evening. He opened a book and showed her that there were numbers inside, just like the numbers on the face of the clock. They would tell her which side of the book was up and which was down. Nobody had ever told her this before. After that, she took out all the books, wiped them carefully, and put them back the right way. Miss Kitty saw her doing it, but did not say anything.

Sahib had been sad since the guest left. He roamed from room to room with his hands in his pockets. One day, he stopped in front of the mirror in the corridor and looked at himself for a long time. He must not have liked what he saw because he took the mirror down and told her to put it in the box room. Sometimes he walked up and down the garden, whistling to himself. Or sat in a chair in the verandah, listening to music till the early hours of the morning.

A savage wind blew in from the west. It brought with it the sound of pillage and the smell of plunder. Drums beat steadily on the tiled roof above. Doors slammed and windows swung madly on their hinges. She ran through the house and managed to fasten all but one. Picking her way through the broken glass, she stood at the empty window frame and looked out. Hailstones the size of quail's eggs hurtled from the sky and bounced off the ground. A large limb ripped free from the trunk of the sheoli tree. It fell across a bed of lilies, crushing them under its weight. The lawn was littered with semul flowers strewn like bloodied flesh. Hibiscus bushes clung to the earth as their slender arms thrashed helplessly about. Flowerpots were knocked over, spilling their insides onto the driveway. A thick mat of fallen leaves and branches hid the green grass from view.

She watched for an hour, maybe more, till the roof became quiet and the garden still. Then she got to work – sweeping, mopping, wiping. Her movements were slow and clumsy. More than once, she stopped to press cold hands over her hot eyes. This was how she was when Sahib came in.

A wave of relief cut through her noisy thoughts. She

should have made a sound or said something, but she did neither. He sat on the edge of the bed with his back to her, removing first his shoes, then his socks. Pushing his shoes under the bed. Shaking out his socks and tucking them into his shoes. One by one, he undid the buttons of his tunic and laid it neatly on the bed. Still she lingered. If only she could stay. Just a little while longer. He lay down with his hands behind his head and closed his eyes.

After a few minutes, he said that she should go.

Birju's daughter Soni was back. Her story was shocking. She had gone to fetch broom grass from the gullies coming down from the jungle. The better clumps had already been cut. So she went east towards the riverbank. There was plenty of broom grass growing there. On the way, she heard voices and stopped. About twenty men were sitting in a clearing. She did not recognise any of them. So she quickly climbed a bahera tree and hid in its branches. From there she saw that two men were standing with their backs to the rest, like guards. The others were arguing. One of them picked up a stick and drew something on the ground. Then they argued some more. After a while, the one with the stick stood up and raised his hands. It looked like he was the leader. Then they all settled down. Except for one of the guards, who walked right up to the bahera tree. He leaned against its trunk and lit a bidi. Through the leaves and the smoke, she saw that he was just a boy. She did not move.

All night long, Soni sat in the tree, too scared to climb down. The men had gone off in different directions. The jungle was dark. They could be anywhere. When the sun came out, she walked along the river till she reached the road to Pipli. It was evening by the time she got home. Some people believed her story, others said she had made it up. Ayah asked Latif what he thought.

Latif wiped his eyes with the back of his hand. 'Who cares what I think?'

Ayah told him that she did, or she would not have asked.

'Those men were revolutionaries. They have to meet secretly in the jungle, otherwise informers will report them to the police. They are making plans. When the time is right, they will strike.' He threw a heap of chopped onions into a pan sputtering on the stove. 'It won't be long. Any fool can tell. The signs are there, everywhere.'

'And then?'

'And then they will drive out the firangis. White people have ruled us for too long. They should go back to where they came from.'

She was surprised. Latif had never talked like this before. 'And what about us?'

'What about us? I'll still be a cook, you'll still be an ayah.'

'But we'll be better off, won't we?'

'How do I know? Maybe we will, maybe we won't.' The smell of burnt onions filled the kitchen. 'Don't you have any work? Look what you made me do.'

Latif emptied a bowl of water into the pot. His scowling face disappeared in a cloud of steam.

Ayah did not take offence. The important thing was that the girl had come back. Maybe it was a sign.

The chatter of birds woke her. At first, she thought it was morning. But the warmth in the air told her that the sun was on its way down, not up. If it was not for the birds, she would have slept on.

A few more minutes and dusk would fall. Ayah quickly combed her hair, hoping she was not too late. Miss Kitty did not like to be kept waiting. She was going for a fancy dress party in the evening. For many days she had been uncertain about what to wear. Finally she decided to put on her big black boots and go as a cat. She had asked her to come early and fasten her tail.

A babbler beckoned cheekily from the open window. She bowed her head and folded her hands. The elders of her clan said that the untidy grey bird was like their kin. Long, long ago, when their ancestor was dying of thirst in the jungle, a babbler had guided him to water. She put down the comb, took a fistful of rice and hurried out.

Six babblers were hopping about under the pomegranate tree. One pounced on another, and the rest joined in with raucous cries. When the dust had settled, a seventh emerged from the surrounding weeds. Carrying a dry twig in its yellow beak, it flew up to the tree and disappeared among the leaves. Its nest was cleverly hidden from view. When it returned, the others were squabbling again. It rushed at them with flapping wings and was greeted with a chorus of hoarse shrieks.

She scattered the rice and turned to go. It was only then she noticed that the pomegranate tree was in bloom. Latif must be right – it would not be long. The signs were there. Everywhere.

18
Kitty

Sharp at half past ten, Kitty knocked on the stationmaster's front door. She felt like a schoolgirl summoned to the principal's office for a misdemeanour, and wondered what it could be. Her cardigan was uncomfortably tight. She undid the top three buttons and straightened the Peter Pan collar of her dress. After waiting a while, she knocked again. A window was open, its floral curtain parted. She peered in. Nobody seemed to be about. Quelling her desire to dash back home, she headed round to the back of the bungalow.

The church had been packed for the memorial service. Madman Morris was much loved and admired. Mourners had poured in from as far away as Delhi junction, each with a stirring story to tell. By the time Kitty made it there, the only vacant space was next to Mrs Lazarus. She sat down and pretended not to notice Ester Llewellyn sitting in the pew directly behind. The stories were all similar but were told differently by retired engine drivers, firemen, cleaners and guards. Apparently old Mr Morris used to address his engine as 'Milady' and for him she ran as for no other man. He knew his route so well that he could have easily driven blindfolded. He won every race against every other driver, and invariably with minutes to spare. No matter what trouble he might encounter en route, his train was never ever late. Also known as SK Morris, with S standing for 'speed' and K for 'king', he had the best safety record of all time.

Halfway through the lengthy service, Mrs Lazarus leaned over and asked her when she was going back to St Anne's. Kitty whispered that she was not, and ignored Ester's noisy intake of breath. That was when the stationmaster's wife had told her to drop by the next morning.

Two men and a cow were standing near the kitchen steps. Just as she turned the corner, Mavis Lazarus appeared in the doorway and waved to her. Kitty skirted the cow and went to stand beside her. The cook handed Mrs Lazarus a clean pail for inspection. The milkman crouched under the cow and pulled gently at her udders. She did not seem to mind parting with the milk meant for her calf. Every now and then, she turned her head to observe how things were coming along. The rhythmic squirt of milk produced a steadily rising foam. The cow swished her tail to flick away the flies. When the pail was almost full, the milkman handed it to the cook and patted the cow on her plump rump. The cook measured out the milk, Mrs Lazarus counted out the change, and the milkman went off with the cow.

The stationmaster's bungalow was just like everyone else's, only bigger. A grand piano lorded it over the living room, with framed photographs resting on crocheted doilies. Hand-embroidered antimacassars protected the arms and back of the sofa. Assorted headgear hung from a tall rosewood hat-stand in the far corner. A planter's chair stretched its long arms, their well-worn surface evidence of many hours of indolence. Above the mantel was a large picture of the Sacred Heart in the bosom of Jesus. The bleeding heart was encircled by a crown of thorns and surmounted by the cross. On the facing wall was an agreeable scene from the English countryside.

Mrs Lazarus poured Kitty a cup of tea and regarded her thoughtfully. She was dressed in trousers and a large shirt that may have belonged to her husband. It was rumoured that she cut her peppery hair herself. Judging by its untamed state, this was very likely to be true. Quite unlike most stationmasters' wives – specially the English ones – Mavis Lazarus made it a point to mingle. This, and being president of the ladies' association, gave her a good idea of all that went on in the colony.

'Do have a digestive biscuit,' Mrs Lazarus urged, 'we're down to our very last tin of McVities. I just ordered six more, and a dozen corned beef – Peter simply can't do without corned beef. This war has been such a great nuisance, but I really shouldn't complain. Thank god we don't have rationing here, like they do back home. Can you imagine living on food coupons? And counting every sausage you eat? If you have enough coupons for sausages in the first place. I hear that these days, if you have a pig, you must give half of it to the government. What the government does with half a pig, I have no idea. Anyway, most people can't afford to rear a pig, that's why they're forming pig clubs, it works out cheaper. Families pool money, buy a pig and feed it table scraps. But then you have to give up your meat coupons.'

Kitty tried not to laugh.

'But that's neither here nor there.' Helping herself to a biscuit, Mrs Lazarus remarked, 'You remind me so much of my daughter Lucy.'

Kitty felt flattered. She glanced towards the piano. The Lazarus children had grown up and gone away some years ago.

'Where is she now?'

Mrs Lazarus said that Lucy lived in Madras with her husband, who was in the Customs department. They were expecting their first child. 'It took her a while to settle down, though. She was a very restless girl.'

Lucy did not sound like her at all. But it would be rude to interrupt and say so.

'To tell you the truth, I was afraid she would never settle down. She was always distracted by things outside. When we were posted in Allahabad, she got mixed up with the wrong sort of people. That's why Peter asked for a transfer here. We thought it was better to be in a quiet place, far from the city. We were right, as it turned out.'

Kitty could not imagine why anyone would choose to come to Pipli of all places. Perhaps Lucy had got mixed up with some boozing, philandering low-life. That would explain it.

'It's so important to be among your own people, your own community. That's how you preserve your customs, your culture, don't you think?'

Kitty agreed readily.

'But that's neither here nor there. Tell me, what's all this about leaving St Anne's?'

Kitty explained that St Anne's had only hired her for a year.

Mrs Lazarus said that she had studied at Oak Grove and it was a marvellous school. 'Of course, in my time, most of the teachers at OG were British. All the girls in my class were Anglo Indian, though I do remember there were three European girls in my older sister's class. Now I'm told that local girls go there too. Only from the best families, naturally – maharajas, senior civil servants, army officers.' She advised Kitty to apply to Oak Grove, and offered to put in a word for her with the principal.

Both teacups were empty. It was time to go. Kitty thanked her hostess and stood up.

Mrs Lazarus took her hand and patted it fondly. Still holding it, she said, 'I believe you met the assistant stationmaster again.'

Kitty flushed. It was not as though she had wanted to meet Chuckerbutty again. But poor Ayah had been dragging herself about the house with a long face and getting on her nerves. And after the bookshelf incident, she could not, in all fairness, put it off any longer.

This time, she had only stayed a minute. Chuckerbutty made a great show of looking for the telegram from his friend – opening and closing drawers and riffling through papers on his table – before finally producing it from his tunic pocket. The message was brief, but he took his time to reveal it, stretching each syllable as far as was humanly possible. In a nutshell, he made a complete ass of himself.

The good news was that Ayah's son's unit was in Rangoon. Ayah should have been happy because there was no fighting there. Instead, she just carried on polishing a silver candlestick as though she had not heard. So much for doing her a good turn.

Kitty decided to say nothing. If Mavis Lazarus was looking to mother someone, she should stick to her wayward daughter Lucy.

The visit to the stationmaster's bungalow made her feel dirty. She had forgotten what the railway colony was like, how nosy everyone was. Nobody had the right to tick her off like that. She was old enough to know what she was doing. It was not as though she had crossed a line. And if she had, it was nobody's business but her own.

Hours later, Kitty was still bugged. Talking to Emily would have helped, but she was not around. When Emily was bugged, she would talk to her mother. Mrs Llewellyn was such a sensible sort. Mavis Lazarus, on the other hand, was nothing but an interfering old cat. Kitty decided she would apply to Oak Grove, and to every other school in the country. Any place was better than Pipli railway colony with its busybodies and spies.

Annie Riddle had been a sensible sort too. Kitty gathered as much from the many things her father did not say. Although he might not always speak his mind, she always knew what he was thinking. An inflection in his voice, a frown about his eyes, or the drumming of his fingers would give him away. She knew, for instance, that he was perfectly delighted when she first told him that she wanted to teach. Despite the fact that he had turned away with a few gruff words.

Teaching was in her blood, there was no doubt about that. Her mother had been so keen on it that she even planned to start a school of her own. Frank Hoffman had said it was the obvious thing for her to do.

Kitty opened the door of the box room. It squeaked in protest. This was where she had come with the primer that Frank gave her. She had shoved it into a trunk of books and toys from her childhood. Now she fished it out and ran through it, letter by letter, page by page. Although she could not read the script, she knew the Hindi word for pomegranate, mango, tamarind, owl, wool, spectacles, woman, pigeon, rabbit, cow, ship and duck. As she traced a forefinger over the squiggly letters with their intricate loops and flourishes, Kitty could almost feel her mother's breath tickling her ear.

But then, blood did not account for everything. Did it?

19
Ayah

'My son is in Rangoon.'

The first time she had said it, it sounded untrue. She said it to herself a few more times till it came out right. Latif was halfway up the jackfruit tree. Its trunk was studded with the giant fruit. He did not trust the gardener to pick a good one. So he had climbed the ladder, asking Ayah to hold it steady.

'My son is in Rangoon,' she told Latif.

'A very fine place,' he said, 'just like London.'

Ayah was pleased to hear this.

'Wide roads, big buildings,' he continued, climbing higher, 'parks, lakes, temples made of gold.'

'Of gold!'

'I didn't believe it till I saw them with my own eyes.'

'You went to Rangoon?'

'For two months I was there. I went with my first sahib. He was a big railway officer, very fat, very white, the veins showed through his skin. We took a boat from

Chittagong.' His head disappeared among the glossy leaves. 'It's full of Indians.'

She noticed that his muscled legs had hardly any hair. 'I didn't know that.'

Latif said that there were hundreds of Madrasis and Bengalis in Rangoon. And Chinamen. 'I bought a ruby from a Chinaman.' He tapped a jackfruit firmly and pressed his thumbs into its spines. 'A big one, the size of a lizard's egg.'

She had never seen a ruby. Maybe her son would bring one back with him.

'Turned out to be coloured glass. Chinamen are cheats. Never trust them.'

Ayah laughed. Latif never trusted anyone. He pulled the dao from his waistband and cut through the thick stem. Holding the stout fruit under one arm, he started to descend. She let go of the ladder. Latif let out a yell.

'Give me a seer or I'm off.'

'A seer! Are you crazy?'

'I'm going,' she sang out gaily.

'A quarter!'

A quarter seer would be nothing once the thick peel was removed. She took a step back.

'Wait! Half a seer! Not a tola more!'

Half a seer was all she had wanted in the first place. The ladder shook. She put her hands on the side rails and a foot on the lowest rung.

Latif came down at top speed and hacked off one end

of the jackfruit. 'You tribals are crazy,' he muttered as he reluctantly handed it over.

A familiar scent was in the air. She breathed it all morning as she worked in the bungalow. As soon as she was free, she made her way to the railway line. Across the tracks and about a furlong into the jungle was a grove of sal trees. They stood strong and proud, their outstretched branches adorned with yellow-white flowers shaped like stars. The villagers in Mitali would be preparing for the Baha festival. They would collect the sal flowers and heap them before the deity in the sacred grove. The priest would offer prayers and sacrifice a goat and a few chickens. He would go from house to house to purify every front door with dung, and the women of the house would wash his feet. The festivities would continue for three days – singing and dancing to the strains of flutes and pipes and the rhythm of drums and cymbals. From the lower-most branches, she plucked as many sprigs as the end of her sari could hold.

When she reached the outhouse of B-6, Bela was not yet back in the bungalow. She settled down outside her door and waited. Bela returned soon after, sniffing as she approached, and exclaiming in pleasure. The two women made their way through the back lanes to B-15 with flowers in their hair.

Bela had left Mitali soon after she was punished for

having lain with a tonga driver from Pipli. No one would have said anything if he was from their community, but he was a plainsman, an outsider. The village assembly met and discussed her case. She would be pardoned if she acknowledged her offence and agreed to pay a fine. Bela refused to do either. From that day, nobody from the village was permitted to talk to her, eat with her, or help her in any way.

'My son is in Rangoon,' Ayah told her. 'It's a very beautiful country with many Chinese people.'

'Really?' asked Bela.

'Rubies are cheap there. If he brings one back, I'll show it to you.'

'I've never seen a ruby. You can get it set in a ring or a pendant. When is he coming?'

'Soon,' Ayah said. 'By the time he comes, we'll have enough money to pay the moneylender and get our land back.'

'Will you go back to Mitali then?'

Ayah avoided Bela's eyes. 'Have some more rice.'

Bela scraped a little rice onto her sal-leaf plate and helped herself to some jackfruit curry. 'I don't miss Mitali, not at all.'

'No. Why should you?'

'I'm very happy here. My man loves me.'

To have the love of a man was good. But it was not everything.

'The little baba loves me too.'

Ayah did not remind her that the little baba was

someone else's child. One day he would go away, to another railway colony, another ayah.

'I don't belong there any more.'

Mitali was her home, she would always belong there. Even after she had been shamed in front of the entire tribe.

Since Bela would not mend her ways, the second assistant of the headman had visited all the villages in the neighbourhood, carrying a sal branch stripped of all but five leaves. Wherever he went, he told people about Bela and invited them to attend the ceremony to shame her. Five days later, hundreds gathered in front of Bela's house. The headman held a sal branch from which a soiled leaf-plate, a worn-out broom and a burnt piece of wood hung. Two sal leaves dangled from the branch – one folded into a cone to symbolise a penis, the other pinned into a groove to represent a vagina. The branch was stuck into the roof of Bela's house. Lewd songs were sung to mock the lovers. Drummers drummed in a fury and dancers danced in a frenzy. They defiled Bela's house by urinating on the walls of the courtyard, and then left. This was the custom. This was how things were supposed to happen. Even after that, Bela could have asked to be pardoned. Instead, she married the tonga driver from Pipli, found work in the railway colony, and never entered Mitali again.

'I miss my sister. She cried so much when I left. The others don't care about me, but she cares, I know she does.'

Ayah drew the younger woman's head onto her lap and stroked the softness of her cheek. Bela turned her face into the folds of Ayah's sari. She stayed like that for a while.

'Won't your man be waiting?'

'Let him wait,' Bela mumbled sleepily, 'it's good for him.'

The floor was cold and hard beneath her. She tried to change her position, but was pinned down by the weight of Bela's head. Settling against the wall, she leaned her head back and stretched her toes. The tonga driver from Pipli was a good man. But no man was worth giving up one's home for.

20
Terrence

When Singapore fell, Terrence was well aware that tough times lay ahead. He decided to take the longer route to his office via the workshop and sidings. That way, he avoided the stationmaster's door. The unwary passerby was liable to be summoned within and it was hard to predict when he would be released.

When Peter Lazarus was in a mood to talk, he did not discriminate between the signals engineer and the tea boy. Everyone knew that it was best to listen attentively and say nothing. However, the storekeeper was new and eager to impress. He took a keen interest in military matters and looked forward to an opportunity to discuss these with the stationmaster. This presented itself when a termite infestation was discovered in the sleeper section. He hurried to Peter with his report.

Peter dealt with the issue with uncharacteristic speed before turning to the fall of Singapore. Unable to restrain himself, the storekeeper offered his own opinion on the subject. With all due respect, he said, it was shocking that such a splendid outpost of the British empire had surrendered after just one week of fighting. Why was it assumed that the attack would come by sea rather than by land? If the jungles of Malaya were indeed as impenetrable as was claimed, how did Japanese troops advance through them so quickly? And what in the world happened to the air support that had been promised?

Peter Lazarus did not appreciate the storekeeper's opinion. He pulled him up for suggesting that the defense of Singapore was not as robust as it should have been. The nation had suffered a grievous blow. The situation called for calm, poise, dignity. This was no time for recrimination. It was time to stand shoulder to shoulder with courage and determination and show that they had what it took to snatch victory from the jaws of defeat.

Lunch hour was over by the time the crestfallen storekeeper emerged. It would be a while before he opened his mouth again.

The mood among the men was subdued. They stopped to swap news as they passed each other in the corridors. Since information was in short supply, the same stories went back and forth, growing in length and breadth along the way. They took extended tea breaks right through the day. Lingering in smoke-filled alcoves, they floated theories and shot them down. Each time a train halted at the station, its driver and guard held forth before a glum audience at either end of the railway platform. By the time the whistle blew and the train pulled out, spirits had sunk a notch lower.

Singapore was a highly lucrative property, a prized territory. It was a symbol of imperial might, a feather in the British cap. Now that might had been dented and the cap was askew. For Anglo Indians who swore by their white ancestors, it was a terrible blow. More so, as it had been inflicted by an enemy dismissed as weak, a race branded as inferior. Who could say what would happen in other battles – to other symbols of imperial might, other feathers in the British cap?

Evidently the men were disturbed by such thoughts. Terrence, however, had other things on his mind.

While going over the quarterly ledger, he had come across a discrepancy in the figures. He rang the bell and told the peon to fetch the accounts clerk. He waited for half an hour. Neither of the two showed up. Irritated, he went to the record room himself and returned with the stock registers. Spreading them out on the table, he began to cross-check the numbers. It would have been easy but for the loud voices outside his door. The penetrating one belonged to the chief trains clerk, Ramaswami. The other was of Babulal, the parcel booking clerk. At first he thought to tick them off, but then decided to let it pass.

'I don't believe you,' snorted Babulal.

'I'm telling you,' said Ramaswami, 'that's exactly how it happened.' The deferential tone that he used before his superiors was gone. In its place was an undeniable note of mirth.

'So they chased them—'

'All the way down the Malay peninsula, 500 miles, no less.'

'On bicycles—'

'Yes, Babulal, on bicycles. They brought 18,000 bicycles with them. Japan used to supply bicycles to Malaya before the war, so spare parts were easily available. The Japanese are very clever people, don't you think?'

'What about food?'

'No problem. The soldiers carried extra rations on their bicycles. And the British had dumped their supplies along the way so they could get away faster. There was plenty to eat.'

'So first they ate their food and then cycled after them? I don't believe you.'

'It may have been the other way around, I can't say. Listen, wait till you hear the best part. So the British blew up roads and bridges as they retreated. But did that stop the Japanese? No, they just picked up their cycles and waded across streams and pedalled their way through villages and jungles. How else do you think they managed to cut them off so quickly?'

'I suppose you could be right.'

'Of course I'm right, Babulal. You should try reading the newspaper some time. The canteen is this way. Where are you going?'

'Where do you think? To buy a cycle – it might come in handy.'

Terrence waited for the laughter to recede before picking up his pen.

British Malaya was a little larger than England. It was mountainous country covered with tropical forests, intersected by rivers and riddled with swamps. Once inhabited by warring tribes, its coastline used to be the stronghold of pirates. In those days, people travelled along the waterways. But science and enterprise changed this. The Europeans pioneered the railways as well as the roads that opened up tin mines and rubber estates for brisk commerce. Just like they did in India.

The south-bound tracks offered a magnificent view of boulder-filled gorges and sheer rock faces — so he had heard. They passed over lofty viaducts and through deep tunnels before descending to more open terrain. The railways even operated their own steam boats and motor launches that ferried cargo and passengers across rivers and streams to connecting trains.

Laying a thousand miles of tracks over steep gradients and unstable soil was a stupendous feat. The first line had opened in 1885. A quarter of a century later, Penang in the north was linked to Johore in the south. Just about ten years ago, a rubble causeway was constructed to connect the mainland of Malaya with the island of Singapore. Over 3,000 feet long and 60 feet wide, it carried two railway lines and a roadway across the sea. It was a sight he had hoped to see for himself.

Thanks to the causeway, trains ran all the way from Singapore to Bangkok. A day would come when they crossed Siam, India, Baluchistan and Persia to arrive at the Strait of Dover. It would not come in his lifetime, this he knew. The fantasy was alluring just the same. But now that Singapore had fallen, what the future held was anybody's guess.

Terrence believed that it was only a matter of time before the situation returned to normal. After all, it was hard for people to dwell upon events that had taken place 2,000 miles away. There were a great many more pressing matters at hand. He was proved right. Trains came and left, goods were received and despatched, passengers alighted and boarded – just as they always had. The financial year was coming to an end. Pending works had to be completed and reports needed to be filed. The men came to work early and stayed on late.

By this time, the branch line no longer existed. Extra labour had been hired to dismantle the final section of track. Lorries plied day and night. The material was sorted and graded. A line that had taken nine months to lay was destroyed in just a few weeks. During those few weeks, repairs on the loop line proceeded exactly as he had planned. Stanley and his men did a fine job. When Terrence travelled with the driver on the footplate for his final inspection, the train chugged smoothly across forest and fields with scarcely a bump. The branch line he once helped to build was no more, but at least some good had come from its demise.

What little gloom remained was finally dispelled by Jimmy Mascarenhas. His knowledge of electrical engineering might be limited, but his inventiveness knew no bounds. One night, he rigged a line leading from the emergency siren to the entrance of the staff toilet. His first victim, the next morning, was Edward Menasse. At half past ten, Menasse pushed open the toilet door. At that very instant, the siren went off. Menasse aborted his mission and dashed towards the stationmaster's office. As was the drill, the men assembled within seconds, and quickly fanned out to check all vital facilities. Everything was found to be in order. Everybody went back to work. Except Dalton, who decided to heed the call of nature. The siren went off again. Once again the staff assembled and once again they dispersed. It was most mysterious. After the commotion was over, Menasse attempted to resume his unfinished business. At the first blast of the siren, he deduced that the two events were related.

Jimmy was a skilled saboteur and it was not easy to detect his handiwork. But when the wiring was finally discovered, it clearly bore his trademark. Peter Lazarus was keen to suspend him on the spot, but Menasse – who had the most reason to be aggrieved – interceded on Jimmy's behalf.

The peace, however, was short-lived. It only held till 8 March, the day that Britain abandoned Rangoon.

21
Ayah

Early that morning, the mali came to trim the hedge. He snipped away like a barber with his giant scissors. When he finished, the hedge was flat on top, like a table. Young shoots and leaves lay strewn on the ground. He tied them up in a big bundle that he emptied in the back lane. They would lie there for a few days. He would burn them when they were dry.

She did not like the mali. He talked as if he knew everyone and everything. It was true that he knew a lot. He got all the gossip from the servants in the outhouses and the peons in the offices. But he also made up plenty of stories on his own. Latif was friendly with him and always offered him tea. He did not take any himself. Instead, he quietly drank up everything that the gardener said.

Ayah stayed away from the two men, but passed by a few times, just to catch a few words here and there. The mali told Latif that the stationmaster's wife had begged him to get some fancy plants from Ramgarh cantonment.

His brother was a gardener there, so it was easy for him to do. She was very happy when the plants arrived and gave him a brand-new pen as baksheesh. It was of no use to him, but he wore it on his shirt on special occasions. His next story was about Suresh, the milkman. He had told Suresh to send his wife back to her parents' house for a few months if she kept fighting with him. Suresh took his advice and his wife was now behaving herself.

The only news from the office was that Kelia the khalasi was in trouble for talking back to the new assistant stationmaster. Everybody knew that Chakravarty babu was no sahib, there was no use his pretending to be one. If he was not careful, the union would get after him.

As the mali finished his tea, he came to Birju's daughter. Soni, he said, was a liar. Her story about revolutionaries in the jungle was nonsense. She had gone off with a boy from Pipli that night. What else could you expect if you did not keep an eye on your own daughter?

When she heard the word 'Rangoon', Ayah wet a cloth to clean the panes of the kitchen window. According to the mali, the war was about to end. The English army used to be very strong, but now it was weak. It did not have enough ships, or planes, or guns. Its enemies were stronger and smarter. And faster. They could attack anywhere, anytime. And when they did, the English generals would not be able to stop them. In Singapore, they took one look at them and quickly put up their hands. And, in Rangoon, they ran away even before the enemy arrived.

As she latched the kitchen window, Ayah thought this made a lot of sense. There was no point in fighting if you knew that you were going to lose. It was a good thing the war was about to end. Her son would return. They would pay off their debt and get their land back.

It seemed as though even more trains were going east without stopping, but she must be wrong about that. It was not as though she stood on the platform counting all day long. She went whenever she could, sometimes once, sometimes twice. If she could not sleep at night, that was where she went. All the watchmen knew her by now and let her be.

The sweepers arrived with their long brooms at dawn. They worked their way down the platform, stirring up the dust. Then came the bhishti, keeping his head down as he aimed a fine spray from the bulging goatskin bag strapped to his side. He motioned to her to step aside, but she waited till a sprinkling of water fell on her feet. By the time he finished, the ground was dry again, but the smell of damp earth lingered. Once a week, a khalasi dragged out a pipe and let it lie across the platform like a thick black snake. When he turned on the tap, it thrashed about wildly, sending water gushing out in all directions. Once it settled down, he went off to smoke a bidi, coming back now and then to move it. She watched from a distance till the flood abated and puddles formed between the railway tracks.

Most of the time, the platform was empty. Sahibs and babus appeared just before a train arrived and went away after it left. Hardly ever did someone get off the express train. And then it was usually a sahib, who was received by another sahib or a babu. When a sahib got on the train, he was seen off by another sahib or a babu. The platform only filled up for the passenger train. People from the villages came early, sat down and waited. They chatted with each other, ate from small bundles of food, drank from copper lotas, and dozed off on thin pieces of cloth spread on the ground. They did not mind waiting. They were used to it. When the signal went down, they collected their belongings and took hold of their children. They ran from coach to coach, trying to get in while people inside tried to get out. If the coaches were full, the men would somehow push their women and children inside and climb up on the roof. Many people who got off at Pipli wanted to get to the villages in the south. They did not know that the train had stopped going there. While they were deciding what to do, they sat down and waited. They too chatted, ate, drank and dozed. Once they left, the platform was empty again.

A girl on the platform was feeding her baby, whisking away the flies that buzzed around her bare breast. The baby kept turning its face away. She kept pushing her nipple back into its mouth.

'It can't breathe,' Ayah pointed out.

The girl stopped whisking and looked down. Her breast was smothering the baby. She lowered her arm to give it more room. The baby pounced on the nipple and sucked desperately.

'She's always hungry,' the girl complained. 'All day and all night.'

'Babies are like that.'

The girl nodded. 'I'm always tired. Too tired to eat, to bathe, to sleep.'

Ayah made a sympathetic sound. 'Where are you going?'

'To find work. We heard there's work in Majra. That's where we're going.'

'I know Majra,' Ayah said, 'it's next to my village, Mitali. What work is there?'

The baby's eyes were closed but its lips were moving. 'I don't know for sure. They're building a station for planes to come and go.'

'That can't be. I know Majra. It's a small village. There's no place for planes there.'

'I don't know. That's what we were told.' The girl winced as the baby bit her in its sleep.

'Rub some honey on her gums, it will help.' That was what she used to do when her son was teething. Mitali's forests were full of beehives. People would smoke out the bees and collect the honey. There was enough to last all year round.

After a while, the baby's lips stopped moving. A thin stream of drool dribbled down its cheek. The girl lifted her breast and shoved it back in her blouse. The baby woke up with a start, waved a fist and wailed. The girl sighed. She yanked out the other breast from her blouse and dropped it on the baby's face.

Ayah watched without comment. The girl must be wrong about Majra. Simple village folk would never travel by plane, not in a hundred years.

Two men squatted on the edge of the platform and watched the tracks tremble. A goods train was coming from the east. It coughed and sneezed before wheezing to a halt. The engine rolled on while the open wagons piled high with gunny bags stopped in front of them. A sahib and three babus came forward. Without getting up, the two men shuffled a few paces to the left. The guard came running and unbolted a wagon.

A group of labourers tightened their dhotis, getting ready to unload the wagon. Two climbed up. Together they heaved a gunny bag and lowered it to the man standing on the platform below, his back braced to take its weight. Bending nearly double, he staggered towards the supplies shed. Another took his place at the wagon. The labourers went to and fro, leaving behind a scattered trail of rice. Inching closer, Ayah heard the guard say that this was the last of the shipments from Rangoon.

The rice was for the railway officials in the colony. She counted the bags as they passed by, but gave up when she reached twenty-five.

An hour or so later, the goods train continued on its

westward journey. The sahib and three babus went back to their offices. The seven labourers dusted themselves off and left.

'So much rice,' she remarked.

One of the squatting men hawked and spat. His spittle sailed through the air before landing on the tracks. The other picked up a few grains of rice and rubbed them in his palm. 'Good quality too,' he said.

'As if that will help us,' the first man observed. 'For us, it's a bad year.'

Ayah said she thought the rains had been good that year.

The second man said, 'Good for those who sowed early, not for us. The late showers took us by surprise. I was still reaping my paddy. He was in the middle of threshing.'

'It's a bad year,' the first man repeated. 'In three months' time, every grain of rice will be eaten. Who can afford to buy rice in the market these days? By summer time, our children will be begging in the city.'

She flinched at his terrible words. All this while she had been thinking only about her son, about herself. About the fact that they would get back their land by summer. She had forgotten what summer was like in the village when the rice bins were empty.

Farmers in Mitali must have sown their seed early. They were bound to have carried enough grain to their homes for the next few weeks. And the rest must be safely stored in their courtyards in big bamboo baskets on stilts, plastered with mud and thatched with straw. The man was wrong. It was a good year. It had to be.

22
Chuckerbutty

Usually he picked up the latest issue of *The Railway Magazine* from the staff library. It was published in London and carried stories from around the empire. There were excellent articles on history, operations, engineering and commerce. What he liked best were the illustrated interviews, the personal accounts, the obituaries. They made him feel as though he knew these important people, as though he was one of them. He read aloud, forcing his tongue to wrestle with names like Geoffrey McPherson and Hugh Devereaux. Originally a monthly, the magazine had appeared only once in two months after the war started, because of the shortage of paper. Six less issues meant six less weeks of pleasure. Someday, he planned to submit an article to the editor John Alton Kay. Perhaps he would call it 'Reflections of an Indian Gentleman'.

'Is Singhapur anywhere near Singhbhum? Because that's where the groom's family is from.' Chuckerbutty laughed out loud. It was the best joke he had heard in years.

This time he borrowed *Constable's Hand Atlas of India*. Burma was shaped like a kite, with its upper sides bordering India in the west and China in the east, while the lower sides ran along the Bay of Bengal and Siam. Its tail – almost as long as the mainland itself – was attached near Rangoon and descended together with Siam to where the two met Malaya. He traced a straight line from Rangoon to Mandalay, half-way up the kite. By a quick mental calculation, it was about 400 miles. How long would it take the Japanese troops to reach Mandalay? The shortest route cut through paddy fields, swamps and forests. Invading troops would not go that way. Instead, they would travel by the potholed road or by the river route, which was comfortable but slow.

The Irrawaddy was untamed, with neither weirs nor locks to control its flow. During the monsoon, the river swelled and its level could rise by as much as 50 feet. There were no charts to guide ships clear of the shifting sand bed. In 1919, a ship had run aground. Since the captain could not abandon it, he had to stay right there till the next monsoon. It took an experienced crew to safely navigate the waters, and the Japanese would not have such crews.

The Irrawaddy Flotilla Company did. It owned over 600 vessels, including paddle steamers, tug boats and barges. These were built in Scotland and reassembled in the Rangoon boatyards. The largest class of vessel was 350 feet long and could carry 4,000 people, even more than the *RMS Titanic* could. Specially designed oil barges carried crude oil to refineries owned by the Burmah Oil Company. And specially designed paddy boats carried consignments of grain to Rangoon, from where it was shipped to Malaya – and to India. Burmese rice fed a lot of Indians every year, more so in times of scarcity.

His father had told him stories of elegant ladies and gentlemen dancing and dining on luxury cruises. Of elephants, marble Buddhas and silk transported downstream – and motor cars, sewing machines and crates of whisky taken upriver. Of eccentric captains and hardy lascars. And of life in Mandalay in the company of colleagues who were as close to him as brothers. He was not alone. He was not helpless. Whatever difficulties lay ahead, he would be able to overcome them.

It was getting warm. He knew by now that Miss Riddle hardly ever left her house during the day. Maybe she would come out in the evening when it was cooler. By that time, the binoculars gifted by her father would be of no use. On three occasions, he had seen her walk down the lane in front of her house, pass through the gate of the railway colony and turn right towards the post office. There, a banyan tree hid her from view. He had waited until she emerged a few minutes later and watched till she reached home safely.

Chuckerbutty decided that there was no harm in visiting the post office himself. It was, in fact, a good way to keep the postal staff alert. All it required was fifteen minutes of his time.

The postmaster jumped out of his chair and offered it to him. 'I would have come to you, babu, why did you bother yourself?'

Chuckerbutty sat down and looked at his watch.

'Sir, will you have tea or milk? Or buttermilk? It is good to have buttermilk on a hot day like this.'

'Nothing, no need for anything. Besides, I don't have the time.'

The postmaster remained standing at attention.

'So,' Chuckerbutty continued, 'how are things?'

'Things are very fine, sir. However, I regret to inform you that there is no mail for you this morning.'

For the second time that morning, Chuckerbutty laughed.

Over the next few days, he wrote dozens of letters – to the head office of the Irrawaddy Flotilla Company in Glasgow and its offices in Rangoon and Calcutta, to his mother and sister, and to all his friends. Once that was done, he sent for mail-order catalogues for an assortment of products that he had no use for. The following week, he dropped in at the post office soon after the mail train arrived. The postmaster made it a point to have the mail sorted as quickly as possible. It was a pity that Miss Riddle did not visit the post office any day that week.

The next week, he got a letter from his sister Tuk-tuk. She said that Calcutta was full of refugees from Burma. They were ragged and diseased. Some had managed to board the overcrowded ships that left Rangoon before the invasion. Others had escaped to smaller ports up the shoreline and fought for a place on any sort of vessel. They did not dare sail in open waters and kept close to the coast, even though this made their journey much longer. Food and water was short. Those who were lucky survived; the dead were dumped overboard. Now that the sea-route was closed, the only way out was over land. Thousands of people who had been left behind were heading north towards the high mountain passes.

Chuckerbutty wrote back to say that she must not worry about their father. Mandalay was very well guarded. The Burmah Oil Company had flown out its officers from the airfield at Magwe. The Irrawaddy Flotilla Company would surely evacuate its staff one way or the other before the situation got dangerous.

As he carried the letter to the post office, Miss Riddle was on her way out. It was strange how fate kept bringing them together. She was looking down as she walked. He noticed that her sandals matched the colour of her hair. Also that she had very small feet.

'Good morning,' he said, waiting till she was six feet away.

Miss Riddle looked surprised to see him there at that time of the day. Shielding her eyes from the sun, she greeted him, but did not stop. She was clearly a very shy person.

'Unfortunately, Miss Riddle, there is no longer any mail service from Rangoon.' He felt she ought to be given this important information. No doubt she was anxious about her ayah's sepoy son and eager for news of him. 'A mail steamer used to come to Calcutta three times a week, but now the port at Rangoon is closed,' he explained.

'Oh?' she said, without slowing down.

'In any case, the army is retreating. Your ayah's son will be back shortly. Please don't worry,' Chuckerbutty said, pocketing the letter to his sister.

She said she would not.

'My father is coming back too, from Mandalay. He works for the Irrawaddy Flotilla Company. It's a very big company, you must have heard of it.'

Miss Riddle shook her head.

'No? It's a top company. Last year, he was promoted to manager. Everyone respects him there, even the Burmese. You know how the Burmese are – they don't like us Indians. They say we always side with the government against them and take away their jobs, treat them badly. I don't know about others, but my father is not like that. He is very fair, very kind.'

Miss Riddle seemed to be in a hurry to return home. He hurried along after her. Today, her hair was tied up. Damp curls stuck to the back of her neck. They looked like little flowers.

'Even when there were protests and riots in Mandalay, he roamed about the city without a problem. Nobody ever harmed him. Have you been to Calcutta?'

'Yes,' she said, 'many times.' It was good to see that she was losing her shyness in his presence.

'When I was young, he used to take me to Kidderpore Docks. It's about five miles from our house on Shyam Bazar Street. We took the tram and got off at Prinsep Ghat. My father admires James Prinsep very much. He says he was a great man – a great scientist, a great scholar, a great artist. As you know, he was the one who deciphered all those ancient inscriptions from the time of Emperor Ashoka.'

As they passed under the banyan tree, the air was suddenly cool. Miss Riddle patted her forehead with a hanky. He could hear her dress swishing against her legs.

'It's a very popular place in the evening. We went early, before it got crowded. He gave me four annas to buy whatever I liked – jhal muri, puchka, ghoti gorom – I could choose anything I wanted. He sat on the steps and watched the boats go by. Sometimes he took out his notebook – he always carried this particular notebook with him – from his pocket and wrote a few lines. My father is a very fine poet. I myself don't know much about poetry.'

For a moment, he wondered if he was talking too much. But Miss Riddle was listening with a lot of interest, so he continued, 'From Prinsep Ghat we walked to Lascar Memorial, it's not far. You must have been there – it's off Napier Road, just south of the Maidan. It's very special. The people of Calcutta built it as a memorial to eight hundred and ninety-six seamen who died in the First World War. I think they were mostly from Bengal, maybe Assam too. My father says that the First World War should not be called the Great War.'

He had just started telling her an amusing story about Kidderpore Docks when the gate of the railway colony loomed ahead. Miss Riddle smiled. Chuckerbutty forgot what he was about to say, and watched as she ran past the watchman. She must be late for a very important engagement.

23
Kitty

Kitty sneezed violently and blew her nose. Ayah stopped dusting the mantlepiece. She picked up the snotty hanky, left the room, and came back with a clean one. Kitty sniffed. Her head was fuzzy and her eyes watered. She had felt feverish all day long, but when she checked her temperature, it was normal. To catch a cold in the month of April was ridiculous. She would much rather have the flu. At least it sounded as bad as it was. A cold, on the other hand, evoked no sympathy at all.

Ayah handed her a cup with a foul-smelling liquid. It was a concoction she produced whenever Kitty or her father had a cold – a mixture of black pepper, ginger, honey, and a bitter berry that grew wild in the garden. She made a face and swallowed it.

Her life was a mess. It had been a mess ever since Jonathan walked out on her. She had thought she would never get over it, but she had. Almost. But it still hurt when his name popped into her head, which was quite often. She could bury the memories of him, or at least blot them out. It was much harder to untangle their intertwined futures and craft one for herself, by herself.

At first she had written to St Paul's, St Joseph's and Mount Hermon. Like St Anne's, all three schools were in Darjeeling. St Paul's wrote back at once, saying that they had no vacancy. St Joseph's took three weeks merely to inform her that they would keep her application on their files for future reference. And she had no intention of accepting the position of upper kindergarten class teacher — which was what Mount Harmon offered her. After that, she tried her luck at Oak Grove and St George's in Mussoorie, Auckland House in Shimla and Sherwood in Nainital. Her best chance was Oak Grove. They were very likely to view her application kindly because the school had been started by the East Indian Railway. The only thing she did not care for was that it had been recommended to her by Mavis Lazarus.

None of this lot had replied as yet. If she did not hear from one of them soon, she would have to think about schools in the south. It was not what she wanted, but anything was better than rotting away in Pipli.

Latif appeared with a tray and set it on the side table beside her armchair. She bit into a kulkul. It tasted pleasantly of coconut, sugar and ghee. She ate two more before pouring herself a cup of tea. The memory of Chuckerbutty still lingered. He was a bit daft. What on earth did he mean by saying that the Burmese did not like 'us Indians'? Was he referring to himself in the plural? Or did he actually think that she was Indian like him?

Just because she was born and brought up in India did not make her Indian. Surely he knew that? She thought in English and spoke in English. She dressed like the English and behaved like the English. For all practical purposes, she was English. People like her did not take jobs away from Indians, they just happened to be better at them. And when it came to dealing with Indians, they were both fair as well as kind. Any of their servants would confirm this.

Only one kulkul remained. She popped it in her mouth and closed her eyes.

Ever since Dan's aunt moved in with his family, he and Pat had taken to spending long hours at the Riddles'. Pat's father was very strict. He did not allow her to entertain young men in her room with the door shut, not even her fiancé.

It was a miracle that the Morgans had survived the evacuation from Burma. It took them all of March to make their way from Rangoon to Calcutta. Ted Morgan stayed on in Calcutta to settle business matters while Alice Morgan travelled to Pipli with their two children aged five and one. The Morgans had lost everything. They crossed the Burma border barefoot and in rags. Their skin was sallow and still bore signs of nasty cuts and painful bruises. The children – a boy and a little girl – clung to their mother, bursting into tears if she left them for so much as an instant. They had been through hell. God alone knew how long the scars would take to heal.

Kitty had got the whole story from Dan. Even so, it was heartbreaking to hear it first-hand. She was glad of Mrs Snow's company when she visited, for she did not trust herself to say the right thing.

'We waited, we really shouldn't have done that,' Alice Morgan said, 'but Ted had to make arrangements for the tea crates, he's in the tea business. I couldn't take the children on my own, so we waited. Everyone we knew had already left by the time we registered for the next European convoy out of Rangoon. Later, we were told that it was the very last one. Can you imagine? We almost missed it.' Alice shook her head as if to clear it. 'There were quite a few government officials who left their posts and got out even before the evacuation was announced. We knew some of them quite well. I can't understand how they could do a thing like that.'

The boy was scratching an angry sore near his ankle. It looked like an insect bite that had got infected. His mother held both his hands in one of her own and gently rubbed his foot.

Mrs Snow said that it took all sorts.

'From Rangoon to Pagan – I think it was Pagan – by truck was not so bad. We carried our own food and water. Lizzie had her favourite toy, a bunny. She never slept without it and I was at my wit's end when it got lost. At Pagan, we got into riverboats and moved up the Chindwin. We camped in the jungle at night. In the morning, we set off early after a hot cup of tea and kept going till we reached the next camp. For supper there was rice, dhal and tinned sardines. Day after day after day – the same thing. None of us can face a sardine again, I can tell you that.' She tried to laugh, but nobody joined her.

'Daddy fell in the water,' the boy piped up.

'That was funny, wasn't it, darling? Ted was helping the men steer the boat through some rapids. The rest of us were walking along the rocky riverbank. One minute he was standing on the bow, the next minute he was splashing about in the water. They pulled him in at once, but not before he had a good swim. By the time we reached the next camp, he was completely dry – it was that hot. I'll never forget that particular camp. One of the porters found a set of tiger pugmarks nearby. We didn't dare let the children out of our sight – not for a single second.'

'Were there many people with you?' Mrs Snow asked.

'Oh yes! My goodness, there were dozens of us! The company was pretty jolly. Everyone tried to put on a brave face, cheer each other up. That's what kept us going. In the evening we would sing old songs like *Auld Lang Syne* and *It's a Long Way to Tipperary*. Tim took a fancy to *Daisy, Daisy* – didn't you, sweetie?'

Tim pulled his thumb out of his mouth and pronounced shyly, 'A bicycle built for two.'

Dan's mother clapped her hands and said, 'That's right, Timmy. And now it's time for your nap, young man. Off you go.' Timmy looked at his mother, who smiled and nodded. She continued talking once he was out of earshot.

'As the days went by, there were fewer and fewer of us left. Half of us had malaria, the other half had dysentery – poor Lizzie had both. Our boat trip ended at Kalewa. From there we had to walk to Tamu. It must have been a hundred miles at least. Every day someone or the other would fall behind. The rest of us kept going. There was nothing else to be done. We told each other they'd catch up, but we knew that they wouldn't. They knew that too. All they hoped for was a decent Christian burial. I don't suppose any of them got it.' Alice Morgan must have told her story umpteen times, but it still brought tears to her eyes. Mrs Snow squeezed her hand.

Kitty felt a lump in her throat. She knew the rest of the story, everyone in the railway colony did. The survivors were picked up by army engineers and ferried to Palel on the Indian side. They showered, had a hot meal, and spent the night in a cattle shed. The next day, a bus took them to Imphal, where the Red Cross provided clean clothing and blankets. Then to Dimapur, where they were put on a train to Calcutta. Loreto Convent had been converted into a makeshift refugee centre. The nuns took in all those who arrived at their doorstep.

The Morgans were admitted to the Burma Ward of Howrah General Hospital and treated for dehydration and exhaustion. Two days later, they were discharged. They were among the lucky ones. The hospital was overflowing with patients with far more serious ailments.

An ayah came in, picked up the sleeping Lizzie and carried her to Dan's room. Alice was left gazing at her empty lap.

'I wonder what happened to our servants,' she mused. 'They were simple Burmese folk and they'd been with us a long time. Ted wanted to bring them back with us, but it wasn't possible. Only Europeans, Anglo Indians and Anglo Burmans were permitted in the convoy. That was the rule.'

'You mean, you just left them there?' Kitty was surprised to hear the sound of her own voice.

Alice looked distressed. 'What else could we do?'

'Don't you worry yourself now,' Mrs Snow said soothingly, 'they'll be fine.' She gave Kitty a reproving look.

Alice did not seem to hear. 'Those last few days in Rangoon were chaos. I hope the poor souls escaped before the Japs got there. I don't think they quite understood what was happening. They weren't scared. They looked quite happy, to tell you the truth. They thought the Japanese had come to liberate them.'

'How very foolish of them,' Mrs Snow observed.

24
Chuckerbutty

Tuk-tuk was right. Hundreds of people were pouring into Calcutta each day. The Burma Evacuees Relief Committee was doing everything possible to help them. The good people of Calcutta – social workers, students, even housewives – were out on the streets, providing food and shelter to the unfortunate souls. Photographs in the newspapers showed clusters of refugees clutching small bundles, lining up to be fed, huddled on railway platforms. They were put on trains that would take them to their villages and mofussil towns, and given pocket money for the journey. Volunteers brought them food and water at stations all along the route.

Newspapers did not report exactly how these people had managed to reach Calcutta in the first place. Most of them were from the labour class. They were more keen to get home safely than to linger and talk to the press about their miseries.

Chuckerbutty's friends filled in the blanks with what

they had heard. It gave him a lot of comfort to learn that the authorities in Burma had organised a series of convoys, each supplied with its own guides as well as guards. At night, they halted in camps where nutritious food, clean water and basic medical care were available. If a person was too old or sick to walk, he could always hire a dhoolie and four coolies to carry him. It was also possible to engage a porter to carry luggage and sundry belongings. If anyone was short of cash, he could sell his possessions to locals in the towns and villages that they passed through. The journey by road, river and jungle was difficult, but all their problems were over once they reached the border. The authorities in India saw to that.

His father was not that old. He was only fifty-five and in good health. He neither drank nor smoked. He ate simple food and never missed his early morning walk. He was both practical and wise. He would manage to reach the border. Of this, there was no doubt at all.

Chuckerbutty was the first to arrive for the meeting. He peered in, saw the empty chairs and stepped out. It was twelve noon. The express had gone through and the passenger train was running late. The platform was deserted except for a woman in a white sari with a red border. He had seen her there a number of times. She must be one of the servants from the railway colony, because she was talking to one of the khalasis. A village woman would not do that. She laughed at something he said. The khalasi strolled away. The woman sat down on the ground next to the bench for Indians.

Within minutes, the other officers arrived. As a courtesy, Chuckerbutty waited for them to file past before he entered the room. He sat down behind Mr Menasse, whose large head blocked the stationmaster's face from view. Peter Lazarus had just begun to speak when Mr Riddle walked in. Chuckerbutty immediately gave up his seat and moved to the lone chair at the back. It was wedged between the door and a large wooden almirah. Now he could see even less. Mr Riddle turned sideways and asked if he had spotted any rare birds lately. Chuckerbutty assured him that he had. For some reason, Miss Riddle did not visit the post office any more. However, just yesterday she had sat on the steps of her front verandah for a few minutes. He flipped open his pad and held his pen poised to take notes.

Peter Lazarus announced that he had called the meeting to discuss air raid precautions and that this was a requirement at all railway establishments. He paused. Nobody said anything. 'As you know,' he continued, 'our country is at war and the enemy is practically at our doorstep. Now, I don't believe even for a second that the Japs will get past our defences, but we must be fully prepared for every eventuality. It's our duty to keep our trains running and to protect railway property at all costs. And,' he added, 'in the unlikely event of a bombing, to deal with the damage and with human casualties — if any — instantly and effectively.'

'Hear, hear,' said signalman James Adams.

'Coming to air raid precautions – I have here this booklet of instructions.' He held it high for all to see. 'It describes every aspect in considerable detail. I expect each of you to read it carefully, and to explain its contents to all those who are not present at this meeting today.'

There was something different about the stationmaster that morning. Usually he took his time to warm up. He talked about this and that before coming to the point. Sometimes he started a long sentence and stopped without finishing it. If nobody completed it for him, he would move on to the next. That was his style. Others might criticise him for it, but Chuckerbutty had always admired the man. A leader showed his true mettle in a time of crisis. This was such a time and Peter Lazarus was clearly in command.

From the first of May, there was going to a blackout every night. Air raid wardens would patrol the streets to ensure that no light was visible from any house or facility. A siren – alternately rising and falling in pitch – would be sounded in the event of an air raid alert. Everyone was expected to drop whatever they were doing, head for a bomb shelter, and stay there till the all-clear signal was given.

There were several murmurs. Someone coughed. Peter Lazarus put up a hand for silence. A peon entered with a tray of teacups. He waved him away and asked for volunteers. 'Men or women to serve as air raid wardens. I'll be issuing helmets and badges to them. Yes?'

Chuckerbutty had stood up. 'Sir, I volunteer.' His voice came out much louder than he intended.

A dozen heads turned. Two dozen eyes stared at him.

'Very commendable, Chuckerbutty, very commendable. But according to regulations, the warden must be at least thirty years of age.'

Chuckerbutty sat down, disappointed. Five men came forward and their names were duly noted.

A common bomb shelter was going to be built at the railway institute. In addition, each family was encouraged to make one, in accordance with recommended specifications, on its own premises, for speedy access. At all times, all bomb shelters were to be stocked with drinking water, non-perishable food and torches. Air raid drills would begin as soon as the shelters were ready.

There were a few questions, all of which the stationmaster answered superbly. 'Right, that's settled then.'

People were already on their feet when the stationmaster spoke again. 'I don't believe I've dismissed you yet.' His words were mild but his tone was not. Everybody sat down. Only he remained standing.

'Now,' Peter said, 'coming to the other matter on my agenda. I'm determined to ensure that we're also prepared for an attack by land.'

'Aren't we getting a little carried away here?' A few heads nodded in agreement with Terrence Riddle. Not Churkerbutty's. He had complete faith in his leader.

'You would not ask that question, Riddle, if you were

familiar with the sequence of events in Singapore — and in Rangoon, for that matter.'

Terrence Riddle muttered that Pipli was neither Singapore nor Rangoon. His voice was low, but it carried.

When it reached him, Peter Lazarus studied each face in turn — that is, except Chuckerbutty's, which was not visible to him. He then disclosed that there was a very strong possibility that Japan was preparing to invade India. Army and naval bases were being strengthened even as he spoke. At the moment, the threat perception was confined to the east coast. It was believed that Japanese troops would not have the necessary supply lines to penetrate the Indian mainland. However, they had underestimated Japan before. And he, for one, was not about to do so again.

'May I also remind you, Riddle, that there are certain misguided sections of the local population who believe that Japan is their friend. They've been fed this balderdash by Indians overseas, who've gone over to the enemy.'

He was right. There was some talk like that. But that was all it was — talk.

'I'm told that there are secret agents operating all over India. They receive their orders from abroad, over the radio, in secret code. You may not be aware of this, Riddle, but there are over fifty thousand secret agents among government officials alone. Fifty thousand, mind you. These secret agents will strike at the opportune moment — when Japan attacks. Surely I need not tell you, of all people, that the railways are their favourite target?'

Fifty thousand was impossible. Peter Lazarus was making a mistake. He must have meant fifty. Indian officials sympathised with the nationalists, but none of them supported revolutionaries. They would never take up arms against the government. They knew full well that the transfer of power was being negotiated at the highest level. It would take place very soon. And it would take place peacefully, without any violence. Freedom would be won with dignity and honour – by all Indians, for all Indians.

'All of us are members of the Auxillary Force. If you recall, it was a condition we agreed to when we were recruited.'

This was news to Chuckerbutty. He could not recall any such condition from when he was recruited.

'According to your personal files, none of you has seen active duty. I have. When I was in Cawnpore, we were called out to assist the police during rioting. A local revolutionary had been arrested and that led to violence in the streets. So yes, I have indeed seen active duty.'

And just like that, the war came to Pipli junction.

25

Terrence

The April sun was hot on his bare back. He stopped digging and straightened up. The muscles in his arms unclenched and his breathing came back to normal. It had been a while since he exerted his body so much. It felt good.

Kitty surveyed the trench. 'Isn't it too big? It says here six-and-a-half by four-and-a-half.' She handed him a tall glass of ginger beer.

Terrence tossed the shovel aside and gestured towards the jackfruit tree. Latif and Ayah were watching from its shade. They had wanted to help, but he decided to build the bomb shelter by himself.

He drained the glass and handed it back to her. The trench was ready. All it needed was a roof of corrugated iron heaped over with earth. Ayah pottered over for a look and offered to plaster the inside with a mixture of cowdung and mud. Kitty made a face. He laughed.

These days, Annie was never far from his thoughts. And memories that he had banished were back in his head.

Annie stood in front of the mirror. He came up from behind and slipped his arms around her waist. His image framed hers – he was a head taller and a foot wider. He pulled her close. She fitted into him snugly. His hands moved up to hold her breasts. She let her head rest against him and covered his hands with her own. Her eyes closed and her skin warmed. It was a perfect moment. Then her hair tickled his nose and he sneezed. The moment was over. She pushed against his chest and went into the bathroom. When she came out, it was in a tightly belted dressing gown.

'Why can't you cut your hair?' he complained. 'It's all over the place. All the other ladies have a bob – or is it called a shingle?'

She ignored him completely and picked up her hairbrush.

'Or tie it up at least. Yesterday it was in the soup.' He knew this would annoy her. It did.

'I happen to like it this way,' she said coldly, 'and – by the way – so does Frank.'

'I'm sure he does. But then, Frank likes everything about you, doesn't he? You should have married him. You know that's what he wanted.'

Annie carried on brushing her hair in long, rhythmic strokes. 'I would have – if you hadn't come along and spoiled everything.'

'So I spoiled everything, did I?'

'You know you did. Chasing after me like that, showing up when I was taking class, begging and pleading.'

'Begging and pleading!'

'Yes, of course, till I took pity on you. It was the Christian thing to do.'

'They say that pity is akin to love.'

'Do they? Frank says the opposite.'

'Then you should have listened to him. He means a lot to you, doesn't he?'

She put down the brush and held his gaze in the mirror. 'It's true, he does. A world without Frank just doesn't make sense. He'll always mean a lot to me, how can he not?'

There was no point trying to get the better of her. She always won, whether by hook or by crook. Annie could be devious, even deceptive. She knew his weaknesses and exploited them shamelessly.

'Although,' she added lightly, almost as an afterthought, 'he isn't my life. You are.'

Annie was his life too. The railways only took over after she was gone.

Terrence stopped saying that the railways were going to the dogs. People could see it for themselves.

The war department had already taken more than a thousand bogies and carriages – on loan, it said. When these would be returned was anybody's guess. At least five hundred stations were now closed to passenger traffic. An even larger number no longer handled freight. Prime workshops had been transferred to the military. Many of those that remained had been ordered to produce parts for shells, grenades, guns and tanks. This was not all. Hundreds of railway hands were busy fashioning articles to clothe, feed, house and transport the fighting forces. As if they had nothing better to do.

Terrence dealt himself another card. He placed the four of spades on the five of diamonds, then added the three of hearts to the duo. He had overlooked the jack of diamonds in the sixth column. Moving it to the ten of diamonds released the missing ace of spades. With it in place, the game came to an end in half a dozen swift moves. He scooped up the cards, shuffled the deck and laid out the tableau again.

All this while, he had been cursing the war for crippling the railways. But the events in Burma told him that the worst was yet to come. Even as the Japanese were closing in on Rangoon, the authorities had put scorched earth measures in motion. Denying the enemy access to vital facilities was supposed to slow it down – that it continued its onward march was a different story. He was well aware that a retreating army must destroy military facilities and equipment before they fell into enemy hands. But the act of denial in Burma went much further.

The oil industry, for one, had been wiped out. Oil wells, oil fields, oil storage tanks and oil refineries were destroyed. Mining installations, power stations and telegraph systems were wrecked. Facilities at the port were demolished. Docks, cranes and derricks were shattered. Ships were sunk at strategic locations to prevent the use of piers by the Japanese. Bridges were blown up. Boats were driven upriver and scuppered by gunning holes into their hulls. According to one newspaper, Britain ended up destroying much more than it had built in its colony.

In the 1840s, a British railway engineer accompanied by three able assistants had surveyed the line from Calcutta to Delhi through Mirzapore. It was to be the very first railway line in India. The plan was to connect the seat of government – Calcutta, in those days – to the distant north-western provinces. The idea was fantastic and there were plenty of naysayers. Yet, the pioneers pushed ahead in conditions that could only be described as treacherous. The floods in Bengal were unusually heavy in those early years. Large bridges near Hooghly, for instance, had to be built on sinking and shifting ground. Ultimately, the critics were proved wrong. There had been no accidents, no failures. It was nothing short of a miracle.

That was how the story of the East India Railway began. He had no desire to speculate about how the story might end.

Terrence pushed open the gate and let it swing shut behind him. A motorcycle roared down the lane. He winced. Its silencer had been removed and the noise was deafening.

It was probably Jimmy with some girl clinging to him on the pillion. He hoped it was not Kitty.

In the five months that she had been home, he had tried not to ask Kitty about her future. Someday she would tell him herself.

Kitty had never been one for planning ahead. He could not say that she was impulsive. More often than not, there was a kernel of good sense in what she did. Though at times this might seem obscure, she always managed to land on her feet, like a cat. He could not put this down to luck, for luck tended to be as fickle as the weather. Nor could he chalk it up to sound advice, because Kitty preferred to trust her own instincts and did not take kindly to instruction. This was no surprise. He had always intended that she should know her mind, make her own choices, take her own decisions. If that made her unpredictable, he could hardly complain.

26
Chuckerbutty

Far from being afraid, Chuckerbutty was filled with a new sense of purpose. There was nothing like a war to get people to put their heads and hearts together. Although he had not been assigned any official role in the defence of Pipli junction, there was plenty for a responsible railwayman to do. Being the only officer in the barracks, he decided to take charge. He got the staff to fix cardboard on window panes, fasten conical shields on lamp posts, dig trenches and fortify them with sandbags. During drills, the men followed every instruction at top speed. The air raid wardens who took turns at the night patrol were impressed. He had every reason to be proud of himself.

Mandalay fell on 1 May. The evacuation of civilians from Burma continued. There was still no news of his father. By now, everyone in the barracks knew this. He had mentioned it one night while sitting idle in a trench during an air raid drill. Others had family in Burma too.

They too were waiting to hear from them. And all this while he had thought he had nothing in common with the staff.

Ever since the stationmaster spoke of secret agents among the government employees, Chuckerbutty had remained alert to suspicious activities of any kind. He paid special attention to gossip, even encouraging the staff to speak freely in his presence. At first they hesitated because he had rebuked them for loose talk in the past. But they opened up after a few nights in the trenches. Many of their stories were about females – this was only natural. In order to win the men's trust, he told a few tall tales himself. Although the more lustful ones were less believable, they certainly helped to pass the time.

Mimicking the officers was another popular pastime. He could not bring himself to mimic his colleagues, but took care to laugh along with the others. Politics was the other favourite topic. To his surprise, the men knew more about what was happening in the country – and in the world – than he did. He relied on newspapers; they relied on word of mouth. Each of them had a view on all that was going on, but so far nobody had said anything seditious. The most vocal among them was one of the khalasis – a man who was otherwise silent. The quiet ones were always the most dangerous. Chuckerbutty decided to keep an eye on him. There would be no revolutionary activity in the barracks – not on his watch.

Krishna salaamed him and ordered a youth to vacate the front bench in the far corner. That was where Chuckerbutty liked to sit. The youth picked up his plate of laddus and moved to the next table. The tea shop was crowded that evening. The only vacant spot was next to Chuckerbutty. It would stay vacant. That was how he liked it.

Krishna bustled up with steaming tea and pakoras. Chuckerbutty took a sip and grimaced. There was too much sugar. Krishna emptied the glass outside the shack and quickly made another. This time it was all right.

An elderly man entered the tea shop, closing his black umbrella. He looked around for somewhere to sit. Chuckerbutty pretended to be absorbed in a passing tonga. The man mopped his brow with a white handkerchief that he pulled from his trouser pocket. After a moment's hesitation, Chuckerbutty slid a little to his left. The man smiled his thanks and sat down, careful that their shoulders should not touch. Such civility was unusual. The man was obviously educated. He tucked his umbrella under the bench and waited to be served. Krishna was busy arguing with a customer, who insisted that he had been overcharged. The elderly man crossed his legs and rested his hands on the table. They were slender, like those of an artist, or a writer perhaps. Chuckerbutty raised an arm and snapped his fingers. At once, Krishna appeared with a glass of water for his companion. The man smiled again, and placed his order.

'It's very hot today,' he observed. His voice was cultured, like his hands.

Chuckerbutty nodded. 'Even hotter than yesterday. It will stay like this till the monsoon.'

'You live here?'

Chuckerbutty explained how he happened to be in a remote place like Pipli.

'So,' the man said, 'you are a sahib.'

He shook his head modestly. 'No, no, nothing like that. And you are—?'

'People call me a professor, but I think of myself as a student.'

'And you study – what?'

'Life,' he said simply.

Chuckerbutty was amused. 'There isn't much life here.'

'I can see that people are a bit sleepy,' the man said, looking meaningfully towards Krishna, who was yet to serve him, 'but perhaps they will wake up when the time comes.'

Sure enough, Krishna set down a glass of tea before him. The man continued chatting. He was from Deoghar, a town famous for the temple of Lord Baidyanath. Devotees came to worship all year round, but in the month of July their number would swell enormously. Millions walked from Sultanganj to Deoghar – a distance of about 60 miles – carrying water from the Ganga to offer at the temple. The professor was not one of them. Neither was Chuckerbutty, but his mother and father were.

'If we were as devoted to our country as we are to the countless gods and goddesses, we would not be slaves today – don't you think?'

Chuckerbutty could not agree without being disrespectful to his parents. A person at the other end of the bench got up and left. The elderly man shifted a little to his right. Now that there was some space between them, Chuckerbutty got a better look at him. He had misjudged the man's age. Although his hair was grey, his face was young. He could not be more than thirty-five or so. Only a brilliant teacher could be a professor at that age.

The professor asked if he followed politics. Chuckerbutty confessed that he did not.

'I don't blame you.' He took a sip of tea. 'Nobody knows what is really going on these days. Nothing is as it seems.'

'Meaning?'

'Meaning that the British keep saying that they will grant us self-rule, but when and how is a mystery. Our politicians may believe them, but I don't. I think it's just an empty promise, a ploy to force us to cooperate in the war effort, to keep us quiet as long as the war is on.'

'But they will go once the war is over. Everybody says so.'

'Will they? I'm not so sure. Why should they?'

'Because they believe in liberty and justice — that's why they went to war in the first place — isn't it?' It was like being back in a classroom. He had been an excellent student.

The professor raised his eyebrows. 'Liberty and justice for people like themselves, not for us. Why else are they still here?'

'Once the war is over—'

'By then they'll have milked us dry. Should we wait for that to happen? I don't think so.'

'So then?'

'So then,' he said with a mischievous smile, 'I think we should prepare for the final struggle – now – while their defences are down.' He spoke loud enough for the others to hear.

Chuckerbutty was taken aback. The professor looked very respectable, but he was just a troublemaker. Disgusted, he pushed his glass aside and slapped a few coins on the table. Before he could get to his feet, the person sitting behind them spoke up, declaring that he was right.

'Talk, talk, talk – that's all our leaders do. I say we've talked enough. We won't beg for what's ours. We'll fight for it.'

Encouraged by the murmurs of approval around him, the man raised his voice. 'Freedom won't come by begging, it must be taken by force.'

From across the shack, someone pointed out that they were farmers, not fighters.

'I don't know about you,' the man retorted, 'but I'm ready to shed my blood at the altar of my motherland. If you aren't, then keep quiet and let others do their duty.'

'God helps those who help themselves,' said a pious voice.

Others joined in with all sorts of nonsense. They should stop paying taxes, someone said. It was the best way to defy the authorities. So was flouting the ban on public meetings and demonstrations. They could fell trees to block roads and railway tracks, cut telegraph wires, bring down electricity poles. They could also burn down post offices, police posts and railway stations. It was difficult to attack British officials since they were always protected, but their lackeys were easy targets.

The professor tugged at his ear lobes and shook his head ruefully.

27
Ayah

At the first wail of the siren, she leapt up from the mat, clutched her pandhat to her chest, and fled. She collided with a shadowy figure at the entrance to the trench. He dropped his torch and gripped her arms to steady himself. For a moment, her hands were flat on his chest. His skin was warm, so warm that she stepped back at once. Latif appeared from his quarters, and the three of them entered the bomb shelter. Miss Kitty was already there. She looked sleepy and annoyed.

That was the first time. Sahib explained that it was just for practice, nothing to be scared about. Bombs were not going to drop from the sky. After that, she took to sleeping in her sari, even though the May nights were hot. And the next time, she ran a comb through her hair, put on her slippers, latched the door, and walked calmly towards the garden.

Sahib switched on his torch to check the time. Miss Kitty had closed her eyes and was resting her head on his shoulder. His shirt was unbuttoned and he was wearing half-pants, not trousers. The torchlight lit up his face for an instant. And then all was dark again.

The siren was still wailing. It sounded like a pig being slaughtered. The image of thrashing limbs, spurting blood and spilling guts came to her unbidden. Back in the village, all sorts of animals were killed for their meat. But the image that came to her now was human. She thrust it out of her head.

In the very first season, they would need to buy seed from the village merchant. Within days of sowing, the baby shoots would climb out from the earth, pushing their little heads towards the sun. As they suckled from the soil, they would lose their paleness and grow healthy and strong. Once they were a hand-span high, they would be ready to leave the nursery. But, before that, the field must be tilled and levelled, its bunds made firm. The sky would darken. The air would grow heavy. And the promise of new life would be everywhere. When the rain came down, there was no time to be lost. The seedlings had to be transplanted in the flooded fields. For a day or two, they would be still in their new home. Then their stems would fatten and new leaves would spring out eagerly. A carpet of green would creep across the valley like a well-fed python glinting in the sun.

From their very first harvest, she would keep aside a maund of rice. Sahib might like to taste the grain that grew on her land. She and her son would bring it to him. Mitali was not far from Pipli. Maybe she would come again, on her own. She could bring eggs from the hens that she kept in her backyard. Or honey from the beehives that hung from the tall trees behind her hut. It might become difficult to visit him when he got transferred to a station far away. She could send him a letter. If only she knew how to write.

Latif gave her a nudge. The siren had stopped wailing. Miss Kitty stood there with the torch, waiting for her to move aside. Sahib followed Miss Kitty out of the bomb shelter. Ayah followed him. She flushed as the scent of his skin flooded her senses. Grateful for the darkness, she hurried to her room.

That day, Latif was very quiet. He said nothing even when she broke a plate while clearing the table. There was a frown on his lips, but his mouth did not open. When Miss Kitty came to the kitchen to tell him that Master Jimmy's mother wanted to know how he made his guava jelly, he just hunched his back. Master Jimmy said the guava jelly could wait, he had to escape before her father got home. He quickly ran out through the back door and Miss Kitty went back inside.

'Are you sick?' she asked Latif. 'Do you have a fever? A headache? Or is it your stomach?'

The chapatti he was rolling became square instead of round. He peeled it off, pressed the dough into a ball, patted it in flour and started rolling it out again. 'Thirty years I have worked for the sahibs and nobody called me a lackey.'

'So who's calling you one now?'

'Nobody. Nobody you know.' He slapped the chapatti on to the hot griddle.

She asked if it was the cook from B-13. Latif did not get along with him. Or the one from A-4. He had a tongue like a wasp.

He muttered that it was nobody from the colony.

'So, someone from Pipli. You shouldn't go there. You shouldn't listen to those people. What do they know about anything?'

'Don't tell me what I should and shouldn't do.'

It was no use talking to Latif when he was angry. She went into the pantry. The brown paper lining the shelves needed to be changed. She emptied the topmost shelf, moving its contents to the lower one. The paper underneath was in tatters. She folded a fresh sheet and smoothed it down. Latif was very clean – he washed and scrubbed things till they shone – but he did not arrange them nicely.

After a while, Latif came to check what she was doing.

'The other day, I went to buy some betel nuts.'

Raw betel nut was very strong. He chewed it every day, he said it gave him energy. She only took the fermented variety. It was mild, and tasted sweet and cool.

'People were talking. They said it's time for the foreign rulers to go.'

This was true. They had been ruling for a very long time.

'If they don't go quietly on their own, they'll be kicked out.'

There were tins, jars and bottles of all shapes and sizes on the shelves. What was inside, she could not be sure. Whenever Latif needed one, he moved all of them aside before he found it. She decided to put the bottles on the top shelf, the big ones at the back, the short ones in front. The jars went on the middle shelf, and the tins on the bottom one. Latif did not seem to mind.

'Nobody will be able to save their white skins. Anybody who helps them is a traitor – he'll be fixed too.'

'Well,' she pointed out, 'we don't help them.'

'We work for them, we serve them, don't we?'

'You mean our sahibs? I thought you're talking about the other sahibs, the white ones.'

Latif said that sahibs were sahibs – they were all the same. They were all on the same side.

'But you told me that some sahibs are different. You said they look like white people and talk like white people, but inside they are just like us.'

'Who cares what I said? Insides don't matter. Not any more.'

Ayah did not believe him. Sahib was not foreign, he was born here. He would not go and he would not be kicked out. This was his home, this was where he belonged. Latif should not listen to gossip. It never did any good.

'What are they doing?'

'I don't know.' Bela passed her a fistful of pumpkin seeds. She split one between her teeth and flicked out its coat.

'See that one over there – he's very fast. I think he'll win.'

The man Bela was pointing to slowed down and the others behind him caught up. 'It's not a race. They ran like this before the hockey match last year. Remember?' The servants had watched the game from across the southern hedge bordering the field. The other team was from Asansol. It lost.

The men ran right around the field and stopped in front of the goal. Each picked up a hockey stick from a pile kept on the side.

'See? I told you!'

Bela laughed. 'Who am I to talk? Big sisters are always right.'

A stout man came out from under the shade of an imli tree. From a distance, he looked like the stationmaster. The men formed three rows spaced an arm's length apart and held their sticks over their right shoulders. After that, they set off around the field again, but this time they walked.

'Any news about your son?'

'He's on his way,' Ayah told her. 'It's a long journey. It takes time. He didn't send me money this month because he'll soon be here himself.'

As the group passed by, she admired the way they

walked – heads up, backs straight, left arms swinging. Always in line, always in step. Only, those were not hockey sticks over their right shoulders. They were guns.

28
Chuckerbutty

Chuckerbutty looked forward to the nightly blackout. It was a good time for quiet reflection. After doing the rounds of the barracks to ensure that no chink of light was visible on the outside, he stripped down to his underwear and lit a candle. His correspondence file was full, so he started a fresh one. According to the latest letter from Debu, Calcutta was ready for battle. There were soldiers and military vehicles everywhere. The government was taking no chances. The city was tense, but the situation was under control. All those people who had withdrawn their money from the banks were feeling silly now. And the businessmen who had run away a few weeks ago were all thinking of coming back. There was no reason to worry.

Chuckerbutty's mother and sister were fine. Debu visited them every day. His house was just down the lane. It was good to have friends like him. If only there was some news about his father.

The Burma campaign was officially over. General Wavell said that it was a 'disheartening and disappointing business', but the losses were not as high as claimed by the enemy. He said that as much as four-fifths of the forces sent from India – British and Indian combined – had returned. As for the problem of refugees, his words were most reassuring:

> It does seem to me that it is being dealt with as well as it could possibly be. The army is giving every assistance it can. The refugees looked to me tolerably well. They were certainly strong enough to carry heavy loads that I cannot possibly look at, and walk with them. I cannot say that any organisation is perfect, but arrangements have been made to provide them with food and rest. There undoubtedly must be hardship in a large mass evacuation like that. But it did seem to me that a very large number of the refugees and people who were coming out of Burma were in a very good shape.

He read the newspaper report once more before replacing the cutting in his file.

These days, he had breakfast with the chief trains clerk, Ramaswami. He had nothing in common with the man. He was an officer; Ramaswami was staff. He was young; Ramaswami was at least as old as his father. He was from the east; Ramaswami was from the south. He ate meat and fish; Ramaswami was strictly vegetarian. But both were waiting for news from the border. Ramaswami's brother was a clerk in the police commissioner's office in Rangoon. He had not heard from him since the city fell.

If anyone in the office needed advice, Ramaswami was the man to go to. Every chapter of the rule book was stored in his head. He knew how every clause had been administered in the past and how it could be interpreted in the future. While hearing a case, he frowned and pinched his lower lip, deep in thought. Usually he did not need to think for long. But if the case was tricky, he asked for more time. No matter how tricky it was, he was ready with his verdict by the end of the day. He had full confidence in himself.

In the barracks, it was different. He prayed and fasted, consulted astrologers and soothsayers, and wore multiple rings and charms. Even after all that, he was not at peace. He was always anxious, always fearful of impending misfortune – anything from the common cold to the end of the world.

So Chuckerbutty was careful not to mention the professor over breakfast. To be honest, he was angry at himself for not seeing through the bastard sooner. 'People call me a professor, but I think of myself as a student' – what a clever line. He was no mere troublemaker. He was, in fact, a secret agent out to misguide the simple townsfolk of Pipli.

He wondered what had happened after he left the tea

shop. Men liked to talk big, show off in front of others. That was all it was – just talk. None of them was capable of acting on his words. It took brains to block roads, cut telegraph wires, burn down railway stations. From what he had seen, the men drinking tea in Krishna's shack did not have any. Unless they had help – someone who came up with a plan and taught them how to execute it. The professor could be that someone.

Lackeys were easy targets – he had heard someone say this. Every British official had any number of Indian servants. Targeting a servant was a way to send a message to his master. A servant could be threatened, frightened off, leaving his master in difficulty. A servant could even be made to take part in a plot to harm his master. It was true – all these things were easy.

They were too easy for a clever man like the professor. He would aim higher. He would target the British rulers through their Indian civil servants. He would choose to threaten them, frighten them off, make them take part in a plot to harm the government. Pipli railway junction was the perfect place to do this. It was the only government facility in the area. All the others were located many miles away, in the district headquarters.

Strangely excited, he jumped out of bed and paced the small room. The candle on the floor by his bedside was down to a stub. It threw his shadow on the wall – giant, menacing. Peter Lazarus was absolutely right – railway property must be protected at all costs. He blew out the candle and crossed over to the window. Like every other window in the barracks, its panes were blocked with cardboard. He opened it and leaned out. The railway colony was dark. The outlines of bungalows were barely visible. He did not need the starlight to locate Miss Riddle's house. She must be fast asleep, innocent of the danger that lay ahead. Her green eyes were closed, their lashes brushing lightly against her silken skin. As if aware of his gaze, she pushed her golden curls away from her face. Then she turned towards him and slipped a hand under her cheek, just like a little girl. In her sleep, she smiled – that quick curve of the lips that he knew so well.

Taking a shaky breath, he knew that he must speak to the stationmaster at once. The only problem was that his story was full of holes. He did not know the professor's name, nor where he was from. He could not even give a proper description of him. They had been sitting side by side and he had not got a good look at his face. If only he had been more observant. If only he had stayed on.

The inert body was stretched out on a narrow bench. It tumbled off when Chuckerbutty called his name. Krishna sat motionless on the ground, his head bowed. Chuckerbutty shook him by the shoulder. Krishna raised his head slowly and forced his eyes open. They were red. He had been drinking.

'Who died?' he mumbled.

Chuckerbutty flashed his torch around the shack. It looked bigger at night with the tables pushed to the back.

'No milk. No tea.' Krishna shook his head sadly.

'I don't want tea. I want to talk.' He waited for Krishna

to become aware of who his midnight visitor was. Then he continued, 'Four days ago, a man came here, in a shirt and trousers.'

'You did.'

Chuckerbutty agreed. 'After me, a second man in a shirt and trousers came – with an umbrella. Remember?'

He did. 'A very fine umbrella. He wants it back?'

So the professor had forgotten to take his umbrella. Chuckerbutty told Krishna he could keep it.

'A very fine man. He gave me a tip.'

'What is his name? Where is he from?'

'Why ask me? He's your friend, not mine.'

If Krishna had been sober, he would have spoken with more respect. 'He's not my friend.'

'He said he is. He told everyone.'

This was completely unexpected. 'Think,' he urged, 'what else did he say?'

Krishna thought. 'He said you are a big officer. Very important. Very powerful.'

Everyone knew that. 'What else?'

Krishna yawned. 'One of us.' He slapped a mosquito on his leg and flicked away the carcass. 'You are one of us. You are on our side. You will help.' He yawned again.

'Help with what?'

'Anything. Everything.'

'Like?'

'I don't know, I swear I don't. Maybe the others know. Shall I ask?'

Chuckerbutty told him not to bother.

29
Kitty

Kitty leaned over. Shaking with mirth, Jimmy pointed to a bald man peering nervously out of the newspaper. In a furtive whisper he asked, 'Are you afraid ... to raise your hat?'

She did not find the advertisement for Vitex – 'world's best hair grower for both men & women' – particularly amusing, but forced herself to giggle anyway.

Encouraged by this response, Jimmy turned the page. 'Bloody hell! Missed it again!'

'What?'

'Barny and his boys are playing at The Park. All through June.'

Kitty sighed. 'So go.' Jimmy was always dashing off to Calcutta to listen to some band or the other in this hotel or that club. Most of them knew him well by now. They even let him take the mike towards the end of their show.

'No such luck. General Lazarus won't let me. He has cancelled everyone's leave.' Jimmy held his nose to effect a wicked imitation of the stationmaster. '*Nec aspera terrent*! Difficulty be damned! Fall in! Fall out! Diss Miss! You're on your own time now! Foxtrot! Uniform! Charlie! Kilo!'

Jimmy was such a funny boy. She passed the cigarette back to him. He chucked the newspaper at her and took a drag. The sun had gone down, but it was still too hot to go out. Not that anything was happening outside. With nothing better to do, she reached for the newspaper. Indian leaders were giving speeches here and there. In her opinion, they talked far too much. Kwangtung and Kharkov were in the headlines — wherever else they might be. An entire page was devoted to football. It was absurd that so many men should be chasing a ball when the world was at war. A tiny notice in the obit column said that Rudolf Besier was dead. But the only decent play he wrote was *The Barrets of Wimpole Street*, so it was no great loss.

Ignoring the rest of the news, she glanced at the ads. A great many were for medicines and tonics that promised instant cures for all sorts of ailments. Indians were so very gullible. Soap and talcum powder were not far behind — and hair oil, of course. When she was too young to know any better, she had let her ayah oil her hair. How everyone had laughed. In those days, she used to be in stiff pigtails that stuck out of her head like two horns. Belinda May, who lived next door, had insisted on giving her a bob with bangs before she left for St Anne's. It was a good thing that she had. Only local girls had long hair. Even though they came from rich families, they were terribly old-fashioned. A fairly nice lot, no doubt, but one always wondered if they had lice.

'Caution is not cowardice!' The advertisement was for a drug that did not just cure cholera, but prevented it as well. Taking it – the company claimed – was as sensible as leaving the city 'in these war days' for the safety of mofussil towns and villages, which was what a lot of people were doing.

This was not the only ad that played up the war. 'Whether in the laboratory or in field of battle, it is STEEL which helps man in his fight against death and destruction'. Next to these words penned by The Steel Corporation of Bengal Ltd was a sketch of a microscope and a cannon.

The next one was even sillier. 'The whole country today is alive to possible dangers and necessary precautions are being taken. Are you taking the proper precautions to protect your life and your family? You can depend on an EVEREADY flashlight filled with EVEREADY batteries in an emergency. Always keep a spare set of EVEREADY batteries handy – Be prepared!' A turbaned soldier holding a rifle drove this point home.

Mrs Mascarenhas swished in. In her fitted mauve dress with butterfly sleeves, she could easily pass off as Jimmy's sister. He got his good looks from her, also his talent. Mr Mascarenhas was tone-deaf.

'Stop smoking, you two, you'll set the house on fire. Here, give me that.' She plucked the cigarette from Jimmy's fingers, drew the last puff and stubbed it out. 'Listen, I'm going for choir practice. Keep an eye on your brothers, d'you hear? No buzzing off this time, okay?'

'Where's the damn ayah?' Jimmy asked.

'Mind your language, young man. Don't you dare speak like that in front of me. I've sent her to pick up some sheet music from Mrs Lazarus. She'll take her time. Lenny isn't to get his hands on the scissors – I've hidden them under my mattress. And Vinnie is running a temperature. So don't let him play in the tub. I'll be back by supper. There's roast chicken and rosemary potatoes –' She turned to Kitty. 'Do stay, there's plenty.' With a flash of nicely rounded calves, she was gone.

Jimmy keeled over. Kitty continued reading.

The most sinister advice came from the insurance firms. 'War at India's Doors', announced one. 'WHY WORRY? When you are fully covered against death due to air raids and any other enemy action in India under BOMBAY LIFE POLICIES.' How sly. They were using the war to make money. Some people had no shame at all.

The next one said pretty much the same thing. 'A HINDUSTHAN POLICY is your ARP shelter, slit trench, sand bag and baffle wall – all combined in one.' It provided full coverage against death from enemy action, including air raids. Kitty frowned. The blackout every night, the air raid precautions, the daily drill in the hockey field – these were just games that Peter Lazarus had devised so that he could play military commander. Now it looked as though other people were playing too. There was 'ENEMY ACTION & YOU. NO AMBIGUITY.

NO DOUBT... INSURE IMMEDIATELY' – against aerial, naval or other attacks. Kitty stuffed the newspaper under the bed. Was it possible that it was she who had got it wrong? That it was not a game after all? That it was for real? She wondered what these 'other attacks' could be.

'D'you think the Japanese could take India?'

Jimmy grabbed her arm and twisted it behind her back.

'Ouch, let go. You know, like they took Hong Kong and Malaya and Singapore? What are you doing?'

'Jujitsu. I know a few moves myself.' He used his free hand to haul her against his chest.

She squirmed free. 'Come on, Jimmy, I'm serious. Could they?'

'Could who what?' Jimmy pulled at the corners of his eyes and grinned menacingly.

At times like this, she could not help asking herself why she was seeing Jimmy. Jonathan was so different. He was earnest, proper, steady. Everything he did was carefully thought through. That was what hurt the most. He had not ditched her in a huff. He must have thought it over for a long, long time, all the while giving nothing away. Gathering reasons till there was no room for doubt in his mind. Reasons that he did not bother to explain.

Blaming it on the war was not the answer. Emily was right – war did not mean that people stopped living and loving. It should have brought them closer, not torn them apart. His real reasons were different. He should have been straight with her, told her that she was not good enough, that she was wrong for him, that he did not want a life with her. And he should have said this to her face. But he did not have the guts. Jonathan was never much of a fighter.

The arm around her waist tightened. 'No,' he murmured against the side of her neck.

'Why not?'

Jimmy drew back a little. 'Because a piddling little country like that can't take a whopper like this.'

'England did,' she pointed out, 'and Japan is twice the size of England, at least.'

'Really? Nobody told me. So I was wrong. They can. They could.'

'Then what about us?'

'What about us?'

Jimmy could be so dense. 'Don't you see? We've had it if the Japs take over. We're the enemy, just like the Brits are. What do you think they'll do with us?'

Frank Hoffman was locked up when Britain went to war with Germany. Anglo Indians would obviously be locked up if the Japanese took over. Though they were born in India, their loyalty was to Britain – everyone knew this. The Japanese did too. And unlike the British, the Japanese would not go by the book. They did not believe in niceties like fair play. Their internment camps would be hell. Nobody would make it out alive.

'When the Brits go, you silly goose, we go. We've always stood by them. They'll always stand by us. You smell delicious. What soap do you use?'

Kitty kissed him full on the lips. It was a long, fierce

kiss. Jimmy moaned, in pleasure or in protest. She could not care less either way.

Neither of them heard the snip of the scissors till it was too late. Lenny held up a cluster of her chestnut curls before racing away in triumph. That night, he went to bed without supper. So did she.

30
Terrence

When the alarm rang, he let it ring on. Normally its shrillness infuriated him, but not today. Today he was not going for the drill. Nor would he go tomorrow. His neck was stiff and his ribs sore. He was too old for war games. If Peter had a problem with that, he could shove it where he wished. For the last three weeks he had paraded around the hockey field, forced his body into awkward positions, and aimed an antique rifle at an imaginary target.

The stationmaster had placed an indent for ammunition – thankfully, it was yet to arrive. An imbecile like Jimmy was bad enough unarmed. Just the other day, he had bent to tie his shoelaces and brought down a dozen men marching behind him. Another time, he put glue on the forestock of his .303 just to be excused to get cleaned up while the rest of the men did push-ups. As expected, he returned the very minute they were dismissed.

Terrence slipped on a shirt, not bothering with the

buttons. Latif came in with a tea tray. He poured himself a cup and headed to the verandah. Settling back in a cane chair, he sipped it slowly. Presently he became aware of a sombre *coop-coop-coop-coop*, repeated at precisely eight-second intervals. He pictured the crow-pheasant stalking grasshoppers and caterpillars in the undergrowth. As it was joined by a second one in the distance, the morning silence was broken by a medley of *coops*. A coppersmith chose to announce its presence somewhere in the dense foliage of the pipal tree with a firm *tonk … tonk … tonk*. As he shifted his chair to get a better view, a red-whiskered bulbul darted out from among the lantana bushes.

He had rescued a bulbul chick with an injured wing once, when he was at Luckeesarai junction. It became perfectly tame, following him around the house like a dog. That was before he met Annie.

Just beyond the lilies grew a ficus, its trunk and stout branches studded with wild figs. A small party of tiny greenish-yellow birds twittered there excitedly. Until he noticed their white spectacles, he mistook them for bee-eaters. Prancing about like acrobats, peering at the fruit, pouncing on hidden insects – the white-eyes put on quite a show. Too bad he did not have his binoculars handy. If Chuckerbutty was not using them, he would ask for them back.

As the sky lightened, the more daring birds came out into the open. A magpie-robin perched itself on the front gate, its dapper black-and-white form glistening in the slanted rays of the rising sun. From this commanding position, it launched into spirited song, keeping time by tapping its tail. Two hoopoes trotted across the lawn, periodically poking their bills into the earth as they approached the verandah. Their untidy crests were folded as they saw no cause for alarm. They would find few grubs until the monsoon broke. That could happen any day now.

Terrence knew that he was not the first civil servant to take an interest in feathered creatures — there was, in fact, a long line of them. E.C. Stuart Baker, for instance, had edited no less than eight impressive volumes on birds for the series *The Fauna of British India, Including Ceylon and Burma*, while serving as inspector general of police in Assam. The last was published in 1930, or maybe 1931 — the set took up an entire shelf in his bedroom. It was a more scientific work than the books that Oates and Blandford had produced earlier. But that was half a century ago. Eugene Oates was an engineer in the public works department, and W.T. Blandford a government geologist. Blandford must have travelled through the area when he surveyed the Raneegunge coalfields, they were not that far from Pipli junction.

But the man he truly admired was Hume. Allan Octavian Hume was a member of the elite Indian Civil Service. The chap actually undertook expeditions at his own expense and put together a band of hundreds of amateur naturalists scattered across the country. Their sightings and notes were carried in the quarterly journal he had founded, *Stray Feathers*. It was a pity that it had ceased publication after eleven remarkable volumes.

Hume was a maverick. Terrence had heard that his boss had demoted him for being outspoken. People expected him to resign in protest. To their surprise, he chose to stay – long enough to complete the manuscript of *The Game Birds of India*. After retirement, Hume continued to air his radical views, especially on the freedom movement. But nobody imagined that he would became one of the founding members of the Congress party. If a man like Hume could hang on with dignity, so too would he.

He would definitely get his binoculars back.

An hour later, he was still there, the empty cup and saucer resting on his lap. Ayah stepped out, but did not notice him. She was looking out into the garden, arms outstretched, hands resting on the banisters. He observed her as he would a bird, noting the gleam of her tightly bound black hair, a red hibiscus bloom tucked behind her ear. The chocolate brown at the nape of her neck was interrupted by the whiteness of her blouse, only to reappear at the curve of her waist. The loose folds of her sari spanned her back, gathered across her breasts and flowed over her shoulder, where they were fanned out by the hint of a breeze. Dulled by age and frayed at the edges, the fabric screened her contours from view. All he could discern were her arms, burnt by the sun to the shade of ground coffee. Unaware of his scrutiny, she lifted her petticoat, stood on one leg like a stork, and rubbed her other foot along her bare calf. He sketched a mental image of her body – lithe, sinewy, strong.

Startled by the clink of china, she turned, shrieked,

and clamped both hands over her mouth. Her eyes were big and round, not unlike those of a spotted owlet. Continuing to regard her with interest, he held out the cup and saucer.

Ignoring them, she took hold of his wrist. 'You're not sick,' she announced.

'No,' he agreed, 'I'm not.' Her palm was cool on his skin. With his free hand, he turned it over. It was pale, almost as pale as his own. She did not pull it away.

The masala omelette was just the way he liked it – with extra onions and green chillies. Halfway through breakfast, he called out to Latif to make him another. Kitty was fretting about something, he could tell. There was no use asking her what it was. She would spit it out when she was ready. By the time he finished his eggs, she was. He looked at his watch under the table. There was still plenty of time.

'I found this on your dresser,' she said, and pushed it across the table.

The pamphlet had come in the mail a few days ago. His friend Philip was planning to buy land in a new township 40 miles southeast of Ranchi. He had asked if Terrence would be interested.

'Are you interested?'

'Who wouldn't be? Ten thousand acres of farmland, rivers, lakes, hills –'

'But it's so —' she stopped, searching for the right word, 'so primitive. I mean, look at these girls with bobs and boots minding cows, for god's sake. It's not our kind of thing, our kind of life.'

'Take a look at the next page.' McCluskieganj was not without modern amenities. It had European style homes, a church for the believers, a clubhouse, a school, a playground, a provision store, a shop that sold records. It even had a railway station. It was — in fact — not unlike a regular railway colony, with miles of countryside thrown in. 'See? It's not bad at all.'

'Well, we could never stay in a place like that. Never.'

Personally, he fancied a cottage in the hills where neighbours were few and far between. Kitty was more a city girl. While McCluskieganj was no Calcutta, it was no village either. He had enough savings to make a down payment in her name. She would have a place of her own when he was dead and gone, whether she liked it or not. He was not going to be around forever. Whichever way the war went, the colonial days were clearly numbered. Whatever happened, Kitty would be safe in McCluskieganj.

'Why would you even think of buying a place there? We have family in Lancaster, don't we? Isn't that where we'll go when—'

'Not Lancaster, Middlesbrough.' From what he had heard, there was not much left of the city. It was one of the first to be bombed. 'I don't know about that, kitten. It's not as though we know them. We've never even met.

I can't remember when their Christmas cards stopped coming, it was way back.'

'But our roots—'

'We have roots here too, don't we?'

'But—'

'But nothing,' he said firmly. 'Sometimes you have to let go. That's all there is to it.'

He was locking up when the stationmaster strayed into his room. The man did not look well. He was getting on in years and it showed. His belt had slipped below his thickening waist. A slight stoop was evident when he walked. He had stopped combing the wisps of grey hair across his balding pate. But those liver spots were on account of sunburn, not age. He must have come by to remind him to show up for drill the next day.

'Have you heard about Junapore?' Peter said without preamble.

'No, sir,' Terrence replied. 'Did something happen?'

Peter gave a wry laugh. 'You could say that. They're closing it down.'

'For goods traffic?'

'Goods, passengers, both. It's unremunerative, apparently. After putting in twenty-eight years of service, Witherspoon should have been called to HQ, given a heads-up, given time to set his affairs in order, consider his options. Not like this. He deserved better.'

Peter was obviously thinking of himself.

'They wouldn't do that to you, sir.'

'You never know, Riddle, you never know. In peacetime, you took these courtesies for granted. Who knows who is calling the shots these days?' Peter leaned back and ran his fingers up and down the armrest. 'I hope they take into account all the good work I've done.'

Terrence decided not to respond.

'I'd hoped to retire from here. It would be good to go out with all guns blazing – so to speak. That's how I'd like to be remembered. Seven more months, that's all I need.'

If Pipli junction were to close before that, Peter was unlikely to get another posting as stationmaster. Instead, he would be parked somewhere in headquarters, possibly without a desk. From there, he would retire quietly, without any fanfare.

'I'm telling you all this in the strictest confidence, of course. You'll keep it to yourself. Bad for morale.'

'Of course.'

'Let me know if you hear anything.'

Terrence nodded. If indeed there was such a plan, he would be the last to know.

'I'm thinking of inviting the divisional manager to inaugurate the new recreation room. While he's here, we could put on a jolly good parade, show him how it's done. What do you think?'

'I wouldn't do that, sir. It's best to lie low, not attract too much attention.'

Peter stood up. 'Quite right, Riddle. An incident – however minor – is the last thing we need.'

Terrence had seen the best of men fall apart when stripped of position and power. Peter Lazarus was no trailblazer, but he was certainly headed the same way.

'I almost forgot. The ammunition arrived yesterday. Firing practice is at 0700 hours. I know you wouldn't want to miss it.'

31
Kitty

The weather gods chose to step in just when all seemed to be lost. The monsoon was yet to reach Pipli, but it was raining buckets in Burma. The Japanese troops were well and truly stuck in the mud. Trapped by frequent landslips and swollen streams, they were unable to advance any further. In other battle zones, their air power had been smartly cut down to size. So much for being invincible. Hurrah! Hurrah! Hurrah!

Thankfully, this put an end to the nuisance of blackouts and air raid drills. Nobody complained when they were on, but everyone celebrated when they were gone. The institute resumed its tambola evenings and weekly dances. Dates for the annual bridge tournament were pinned up on the noticeboard. Mr Farrow's fortieth birthday party went on all night long. His fussy neighbours did not object at all – they were among the last to leave. After being cooped up in the house after dark, it was lovely to roam the colony at night. Older children were away in boarding school, but the little ones were allowed to stay out late. By the light of lamp posts, they played Marco Polo or pitthoo. Or, led by Lenny, they went from house to house, rang the doorbell and ran away. Nobody seemed to mind that either.

The war was not over, though. The darkened window panes and heavy curtains stayed. So did the bomb shelters. And the morning drill in the hockey field continued. They practised with real bullets now. She could hear the *phitt-phitt-phitt* from way off. Her father was the only one who did not show up.

She turned her head sideways and surveyed the result in the mirror. Her hair still looked like an unmade nest. Pat was sporting a french braid and insisted that her bridesmaids do the same. Normally she could be talked out of anything, but as a bride she was very bossy. She had also said they must wear pink. Emily, who had come down specially for the wedding, was delighted. Kitty was not. She plucked out a dozen pins and dragged a brush through her hair. Her arms were tired and her fingers numb. Giving up, she shouted for Ayah.

A good many minutes later, Ayah ambled in. She clasped her hands to her chest and exclaimed, 'Miss Kitty! So beautiful!'

'Don't be silly. Here,' she said, thrusting the brush at her, 'help me fix this.'

Ayah took the brush and fingered the tangled curls. 'A little bit of oil—'
'No oil.'
'Just—'
'No.'
Ayah subsided and glanced at the picture in the magazine propped on the dressing table. Before Kitty could finish translating the instructions, she had put down the brush and picked up a comb. Deftly, she gathered a strand of hair from the top, then one from the left, then one from the right, all the while murmuring 'so beautiful'. She drew in strand after strand, down to the nape of Kitty's neck.

'Done? So soon?'
'It's easy, just like weaving a mat.'
Kitty turned her head this way and that. She looked sleek, elegant, sophisticated – nothing like herself. Ayah had done a marvellous job. For someone who could not even read her own name, she really was quite clever. It was a pity she had not gone to school.

Ayah replaced the brush and comb and asked when she was getting married.

'Who knows? Not this year for sure.'
'Send for me. I'll come back and make your hair, just like this.'
'Why?' Kitty asked. 'Where will you be?'
Ayah explained that she and her son were going home to their village. Kitty was surprised. All her previous ayahs had left their villages for good. In a way, she would

miss Ayah. Though not as much as her father would. He definitely had a soft corner for her.

'You didn't tell me he's back.'

He was not. Ayah's plan was merely based on a blooming pomegranate tree and a bunch of babblers. The story was long and complicated and made no sense whatsoever. Kitty straightened her sash. Ayah had her own peculiar way of looking at things. She might well be right. The boy could return one of these days.

'And Master Jimmy – he can wait that long?'

Kitty laughed all the way to church.

Pat's father dabbed away at his eyes right through the service, though his daughter was only moving across the street. He would see plenty of her – she had not even bothered to pack a suitcase. Kitty wanted to speak with Emily, but every few minutes, old Mrs Michaels would grip her arm and mutter in her ear. She had something nasty to say about everyone, including the pastor. His hand, she claimed, was in the collections plate. It was a good thing that the couple had such a short engagement. The way they had been carrying on was perfectly disgraceful. Susie Adam's hat was ridiculously large. Stanley McBride would have a heart attack if he did not watch out – it was what killed all the men in his family. Eric Snow's suit smelled of mothballs. Mrs Mascarenhas' bosom was fairly popping out of her dress, showing nothing but her lack of breeding. Kitty, she saved for the very last.

'Pink is not your colour, sweetie,' she whispered.

'I know,' Kitty whispered back, 'neither is it yours.'

Dan's cousins from Bombay were wild. Two of them took over the bar and sprayed the crowd with champagne. They knew the most popular numbers and the latest moves. Turning the music way up, they drove the younger lot out on to the badminton court. It was the perfect place to dance – why had nobody thought of it before? They jived like pros and made terrific instructors. Kitty tossed her head, kicked up her heels, lifted her knees, swung her hips, and let the pounding music take her where it would.

Before the party broke up, Jimmy strapped on his guitar and took the stage. Kitty felt beads of sweat trickle down her spine. Emily fanned herself vigorously with a damp hanky. Jimmy, however, looked cool as a cucumber. At the opening notes of *The Way You Look Tonight*, a sigh rippled through the audience. Even the guests from Bombay were stilled. Each chord so wistful, each word so wishful – Jimmy sang with a tenderness that tugged at the very soul.

Without taking her eyes off him, Emily asked Kitty why he was looking at her like that.

'Like what?'

Emily fluttered her lashes with an exaggerated sigh. Kitty told her to shut up. Judging by the number of heads that turned her way, many were asking themselves the same question.

The next morning, she slept in, waking at noon to the sound of the grass being mowed. Raising her head with some difficulty, she peered out of the window. The lawn mower was being pulled by a massive ox and pushed by a spindly gardener. They were unlikely to finish any time soon. Flinging on her dressing gown, Kitty went to the dining room. Latif had left her lunch on a tray on the dining table. Neither he nor Ayah were about. She picked up the post in the hallway and went back to her room.

Kicking off her slippers, she flopped down on the bed and ripped open the first envelope. It had to be from Oak Grove, the rest had already replied. When her father had said that any school would be happy to have her, she did not believe him. It was the kind of thing that parents were supposed to say. There was really no point in getting her hopes up. It was better to be realistic, practical. But if they rose on their own, she could hardly haul them down.

Hurrah! Hurrah! Hurrah! Her father was right! Oak Grove was one of the best and it wanted her – Katherine Riddle – to teach the seniors, no less. She had better go tell him at once. His anxious sidelong glances had not escaped her. It was time to put him out of his misery.

Mussoorie was at least 500 miles west of Darjeeling. St Anne's would be left way, way behind. She would always remember St Anne's, how could she not? It was her school, her home, for eleven unforgettable years. She had plucked berries from the ivy that draped the school walls and gobbled them up. She could not forget the arches and alcoves, where girls huddled to spill their secrets. The flagstoned path leading to the chapel on which many a shoe got scuffed. The cavernous dorms where naughtiness was the norm, cosy classrooms where lessons were learned. That first, memorable visit to the infirmary. And all those affectionate teachers, who had welcomed her back as one of their own. There was Betsy Wilson who popped in for cocoa at midnight. Sara Cooper, always ready to mind her class when Kitty asked. Even Mrs Peterson, with her outdated notions of suitable literature for young ladies. And how could she forget the motherly Matron, who was determined to dose one and all with a daily spoonful of Waterbury's Compound?

As she got to her feet, the second envelope slid off her lap and lay on the durrie face down. Turning it over, she saw that it had foreign stamps. Jimmy's father would love to have them, he had a fabulous stamp collection. Jimmy kept threatening to sell the rare ones and buy a car. Of course, he was only joking. She needed to steam them off very, very carefully. It was only then that she noticed the handwriting. It was Jonathan's.

32
Ayah

Since the earth refused to yield, she had to force her way in. The blade loosened the soil – gently, so that the roots remained intact. She was pleased that the mali was so lazy. It meant that she could tend the vegetable garden as though it were her own. She gripped the weed by the neck, twisted it halfway, and pulled. After giving it a good shake, she tossed it on the pile behind her. Plenty of ladyfingers were ready to be picked. The gardener would let them grow fat before bringing them around to the kitchen door. Latif would say they were too tough. The mali would then take them home and his wife would fry them for dinner. She snapped a pod in two. No longer than her middle finger, its seeds were soft and sticky.

The pantry door banged and Miss Kitty appeared. Ayah rubbed her hands with earth to clean them.

'I'm going out,' Miss Kitty said.

Ayah nodded. These days, Miss Kitty went out every

evening. Sahib would come home and ask where she was. Latif did not know, neither did she.

'What shall I tell Sahib?'

'Nothing. I'll be back soon.'

She would be late again. Sahib would eat dinner alone.

'Tell Latif to get my shoes fixed, the brown ones. One of the soles came off yesterday.'

'He's not here. I'll take them.'

'They're on the kitchen steps.'

When Miss Kitty turned to go, Ayah pointed out that the brown shoes were on her feet. Miss Kitty looked surprised.

'Never mind then. It can wait.'

'I'll get an umbrella, it's going to rain.' She rushed inside to fetch it, but Miss Kitty was gone. Wherever she was going, it was not with Master Jimmy. The poor boy came to the house every day and each time Miss Kitty was out.

It was not like that before. Master Jimmy used to come quietly from the back gate and ask her if it was safe to enter the house. If Sahib was home, he would go away and come back another time. If Sahib was not at home, he went straight to Miss Kitty's room. Nobody disturbed them. Latif said that if Miss Kitty was his daughter or sister, he would have broken her legs and nobody would have blamed him. People from the plains talked like that. But they would quickly marry off the girl instead of breaking her legs. Finding a match for a lame girl was not easy.

Her people were different. Young girls and boys talked and joked together. They sang and danced at festivals, roamed together at fairs, strolled to the weekly market side by side. If a girl went with a boy into a forest or a field, there was no shame, no dishonour. It was on the second day of cutting thatching grass that she had gone with a boy she would later choose to marry. He was visiting Mitali to help his kin as they had no sons. After he had thatched their roof, he followed her to the stream and took her by the hand. She was fifteen years old. She knew what she was doing. Before the maize filled with milk, they were wed. The bride price was twelve rupees. She entered his hut wearing the special bangle that married women wore. When she left Mitali nine years later, she took it off.

The clang of the front gate told her that Sahib was back. He was home early again. She stopped digging and waited for the music to blow into the garden. He would sit in the verandah and wait for Latif to bring him tea. But Latif had gone to Pipli again. He went often, even though she had told him not to. She did not know what he did there. He always came back empty-handed, but full of anger.

Once, she asked him why he went.

'Mind your business,' he snapped. 'What's it to you?'

She advised him to go put his head under the handpump.

'Don't tell me what to do. Enough people are doing that already.'

'Who?' she asked. 'What are they saying?'

Latif made a mocking sound. 'There's no use telling you anything. You'll never understand.'

'Why won't I understand? I'm not stupid.'

That cooled him down. 'My heart is heavy, that's all.' His shoulders fell and he looked away. 'If you knew how we've been used and abused by white people, your heart would be heavy too.'

Stung by these words, Ayah gave it back to him. 'You think I don't know? White people only came here yesterday. We tribals have been used and abused for centuries. Will that stop when white people go? You and your friends in Pipli don't talk about that, do you?'

Sometimes strangers came to visit Latif at night. She did not hear what they said. It was better that way. Though he looked tired, Latif did not ask her to help him any more. One day, he split open his palm while peeling carrots. The cut was deep, but he did not seem to feel the pain. She took the knife from his hand and peeled the rest. The anger in him was gone. Something else had taken its place. She could not say what it was.

He would be back any minute. She picked up the spade and finished weeding the bed.

Sahib's music blew into the garden. The music of her people was different. When the bamboo flute took its first breath and the pulse of the drum surged through the air, no one could be still. Day or night, at work or at rest, they swayed, they stepped, they swung. But the sweetest sound was that of their song. They sang of the creation of the world, of rivers and forests, animals and birds. They sang in praise of the deities and pleaded for their protection. There were songs of birth and marriage, divorce and death. Every festival – there were so many – began and ended with song. And there were songs for the hunt and songs for the crops.

Clusters of green tomatoes hung low, their stems too weak to hold them high. Reaching into their tangled leaves, she propped them up with dried branches. They were safe until they turned red – then she would have to pluck them before the birds found out. A plump gourd hid itself from view, its skin glowing with good health. Latif might cook it any day if she did not tell him to leave it there for seed. Bad seed could ruin a whole crop. That was what had happened to the brinjals. They came out ugly and twisted, and nobody but the worms wanted to eat them.

Life without song had no meaning for her people. It was their way to know, to sense, to imagine the cool rays of dawn that set the hills on fire. The porcupine hiding behind the ant hill. The glitter of fish in the still waters of a pond. The shriek of the flycatcher nesting in the kadam. The gaze of the horned owl in the moonlight. The paddy weeping for the sky to drench the earth. The pleasure of new ornaments, the tedium of household chores. The teasing of a friend. The worries of a mother.

The shiver of desire. The touch of a lover.

By the time she washed her hands and feet, the clouds had rolled in. The first rain always struck long and hard. Latif would be forced to take shelter under a big tree. She hoped he would get back in time to cook dinner. Lighting the stove, she boiled some water and poured it over a spoonful of leaves in the teapot. Hot milk went into a little jug, and sugar into a bowl of its own. Taking biscuits from a tin in the pantry, she arranged them in a circle on a quarter plate. That just left the strainer, a teaspoon and a napkin. The living room was dark and the gramophone covered. She set the tray down in the shadows of the verandah. Sahib's slippers lay beside his empty chair.

The birds had fallen silent. The leaves had stopped rustling. A streak of lightning split open the black sky above. For less than an instant, the earth was bathed in silver. Then it shuddered as the calm was broken by a savage roar. Beneath her feet, the grass was silken. Rose bushes sheathed their thorns as she brushed past. The jamun tree pointed to a clearing up ahead. The rain waited till she reached there before it came down. The flood that followed numbed her mind, stripping her of reason, of thought. But she knew what she was doing when he took her by the hand.

33

Kitty

The shuttlecock soared high in the air. Kitty waited for it to begin its descent. When it was barely within reach, she slammed it across the net. There was no doubt about it, she was in fine form. Jennifer lunged forward, but could not pick it up. With her hopeless backhand, she did not have a chance.

'Out?'

Jennifer shook her head. Kitty fingered the gut of her racquet and wiped her sweaty hands on the sides of her skirt. Though she tried her best to give Jennifer the next few points, the service kept coming back to her. At this rate, the game would go on forever. She had other things to do. Clearly Jennifer did not. She was tottering about the court like a new-born foal, expecting to find her feet by and by. Kitty had no option but to serve up an ace. A lob on the baseline gave her the next point. She ended the game with a gentle flick across the net.

Jennifer was keen to play again, but Kitty said she

had to go. They returned the racquets and shuttles to the sports room. Jennifer stayed on for carrom with Ben Atkin and his cousin Chris. The three insisted that she join them. It was hard to refuse without appearing rude.

Carrom was not her game. Chris was some sort of champion back in Patna and decided to teach her the finer points of the game. He could not have been more annoying if he tried. When her turn came, he would point out where she should aim and explain why. He even held her hand and crooked her fingers for her. Jennifer and Ben were way ahead, so neither of them cared. Kitty played as badly as she could, but that only encouraged Chris to redouble his efforts. A shot from Ben spun the striker off the board and under the table. She kicked it across the room before the others could see. It was the only way out.

A gentle drizzle was falling by the time she left the institute. There was a bench under the tree by the fishpond. It was wet. She dried a spot with her hanky, sat down, and took Jonathan's letter from her pocket. Though she had read it often enough to recite it from memory, it still left her confused. Nobody else was around. She read aloud to the steady patter of raindrops on lotus leaves. This time, it started to make sense.

It had all started when Baldwin Locomotive Works, an American firm, sent its engineers to the Jamalpur workshop for consultations. Locos were being ordered from America because Britain had stopped supplying them during the war. One of Baldwin's engineers was

Mr Ritter. This Mr Ritter happened to meet Jonathan quite by chance and was very impressed with him. Most people were. Anyway, when Mr Ritter found out that Jonathan was just about finished with his training at Jamalpur, he offered him a job. In America. Jonathan did not believe he was serious. That was why he never mentioned it to her. When Mr Ritter returned to America, he sent an airmail to say that there was a good opening for him if he was willing to join before Christmas.

Christmas was only three weeks away and he had promised to spend it at Pipli. He wanted to talk to her, but everything was happening so fast. There was no time to think, let alone write. Mr Ritter arranged for his passport, visa and passage and before he knew it, he was on the other side of the Atlantic.

Jonathan knew how things must look, especially since she had not answered his telegram. And for that he was terribly sorry. When he joined Baldwin, he had no idea if he would like the work, the place, the people. He also had no idea if they would like him. So there was really no point in writing to her until he was sure about his future. Now that his six-month probation was over, it was the very first thing he was doing.

Eddystone was a little town on the north bank of the Delaware river, bound by creeks to the east and to the west. Jonathan had rented a quaint old cottage with wooden floorboards that creaked as he walked on them. The kitchen was enormous and wild roses climbed up the front porch. A row of shops sold everything from chewing gum to cameras. The neighbours invited him out on weekends. They went fishing, or took a steamer downriver. Or even drove to New York. In the movies, America was big, bold. In reality, it was even better.

Then came the best part – 'Say you'll join me, dearest Kat! Please say you will!'

'Can't you stay? Just a few more days?'

Emily said she could not. 'The hospital is totally swamped and we're short of everything – staff, medicines, even water. May was the worst; more wounded arrived every single day. There weren't enough beds so we made room on the floor – in the wards, the corridors. There's hardly any space left to walk. Not that the boys complain – many don't even know where they are. It's the same in all seven base hospitals. Thank god the last of the troops have been evacuated from Burma. But there's still so much to do. I've got to get back, honest.'

'You're overworked—'

'Everyone is. You can't imagine what it's like, Kit. The heat is unbearable and there's the stench of rotting flesh and piss and shit and puke – everywhere. Most of them are too far gone, all we can do is pray that they die quickly. They die every day – so many of them – faster than they can be buried. You know what we do? We dip a sheet in ice water, wring it out, wrap up the body, and hope that it keeps awhile. The others watch while we do this – they know that any of them could be next. They say it's better than dying out there in the jungle and being eaten by wild animals.'

Kitty could not think of anything to say.

'To tell you the truth, I didn't come for the wedding. I came because I thought I was going mad. I had to get away. I'm fine now.' Emily did not look fine. She looked pinched and worn. 'And –'

'And?'

'They're just boys, Kitty. And they don't even know what they're fighting for.'

'They chose—'

'No, they didn't – nobody chooses this.' She bundled up her hair in quick, fierce moves and jabbed in half a dozen pins. The old Emily would have never gone out in a creased dress without so much as a dash of lipstick. 'There,' she said, 'that's done. Let's go.'

Kitty hesitated. She desperately needed to talk to her about Jonathan, but it was obviously not a good time.

Jonathan had changed. Earlier, he used to write about things that were happening in different parts of the world. His letter from Eddystone did not even mention the war. Instead, it was full of his exciting new life. And, of course, himself. He did not ask how she had got through the last six months, what she had told her friends, whether she was seeing someone else. True, he did say he was sorry. And that he wanted her by his side. But only if she went there. What if she did not? Would he come back for her? Did he love her enough to do that?

'Jonathan?'
She waited for her stomach to flip, the way it always did when she said his name. It did not budge.

As she gathered an armful of lilies in the garden, Kitty watched Ayah go into the bomb shelter. She had a broom in one hand and a duster in the other. There was really no need to keep it clean any more. Somebody ought to have told her. A couple of families had already dismantled theirs. Others had left it as a den for their children to play in.

Nobody had told Ayah that all the troops had left Burma a while ago. By now, the men had sent word to their families that they had made it out alive. There were official aides to help them send a telegram, a postcard, a letter. Ayah had received nothing. If a soldier was wounded, the authorities were duty-bound to notify his family. Ayah had not been notified. This could only mean one thing. Her son was not coming back.

In due course, an official letter would arrive. She would not be able to read it. Someone would have to explain it to her. Ayah would not go back to her village. She would stay on in the railway colony, like all the other ayahs. She would look after other people's children. Though nobody had looked after hers.

Kitty bumped into her father, who was coming down the steps. 'Going somewhere?' she asked.

After a slight hesitation, he shook his head, turned around and walked back inside with her. 'Didn't you say there's a movie at the institute tonight?'

'There is,' she said. 'I changed my mind.'

34
Chuckerbutty

Chuckerbutty lay on his side to lessen contact with the damp bed sheet. He pulled his pillow lower so that the knots in the charpoy no longer pressed painfully into his neck. Outside, it was raining. The very same rain that had interrupted the rescue of refugees from Burma.

When Ramaswami received a telegram from Dimapur, he had left for Assam at once. His prayers were answered, his brother was alive. He was sick, delirious, thin as a stick. Ramaswami had carried him in his arms like a baby because he was unable to walk. He took his brother back home to Madras, stayed for two days, and then let his family care for him. The doctors said he would recover, though it would take time. Ramaswami had promised to make enquiries about Chuckerbutty's father, and he did.

Buddhadeb Chakravarty was stranded in a transit camp on the border, along with hundreds of other refugees. Ramaswami's brother was among the lucky ones – he was picked up just before the roads were washed away by a heavy downpour. The rescue effort would only resume when the monsoon weakened in October. For the next three months, the refugees would have to stay where they were.

Ramaswami brought him sacred ash from Tirupati and told him to place a pinch of it on the tip of his tongue first thing in the morning. He gave him a copper ring and told him to wear it on the middle finger of his left hand. He also taught him a mantra that would ensure the safe return of his father. Chuckerbutty accepted these with profound gratitude. There was a time when he had believed in human justice rather than divine intervention. Not any more. Now it was up to the gods to save his father.

New accounts of the evacuation had come to light. The old stories were lies. The authorities had arranged two routes for refugees to get out of Burma. One had proper facilities for food, shelter and porters. The other did not. The first route was for white people. The second was for black people. Travellers on the white route were escorted across the border as fast as possible. After all, white people were the rulers, they could not be kept waiting. Travellers on the black route were forced to halt many times. Their numbers were far greater, they were more sick and more helpless, but they were less important. They were subjects, they could wait.

They would wait in the transit camps while food and medicine ran out. They would wait till they died of malaria or blackwater fever or maggot-infested sores. When they finished waiting, their bodies would be burned in heaps to save on scarce firewood. Or simply slipped into the river, dropped off the edge of a cliff. Subjects were entitled to neither justice nor humanity.

For the last time, Chuckerbutty picked up the binoculars and carefully wiped the lenses with a soft cloth. It was very kind of Mr Riddle to lend them to him, but now they had to be returned. Standing by the window and gazing at the railway colony had become a habit. It began his morning – like a leisurely walk, for instance, or a strong cup of tea. Some days, all he managed was a quick glance before his bath or breakfast. Evenings were when the place came alive and, if he was lucky, there would be just enough light to watch it happen. In his mind he travelled in space and time, and that night his dreams would appear in colour.

Slipping the leather strap around his neck, he looked through the eyepieces and adjusted the focus. A man in uniform was passing through the north-east gate that led to the station. Like him, he was late for work. Unless they had a very good reason, they were going to be reported. In other government departments, the staff could get away with almost anything. It was not like that in the railways.

A jeep entered the main gate and turned into the driveway of the institute. The driver jumped out and unloaded some boxes, stacked them on one side, and drove away. They could lie there for a month and nobody would steal them. Railway people were honest. Once, he had dropped a four-pice coin near the ticket counter and a coolie had come running to return it. He said that keeping it would be like stealing from his own family. If it belonged to a passenger, it would be a different matter. Chuckerbutty scolded him for saying such a thing, but he knew what the coolie meant.

On Shyam Bazar Street in Calcutta, there was a famous sweet shop owned by a young man named Bishnu Kumar Roy. Everyone called him Beekayda, adding the last two letters that were used to address a brother. People came to buy his rossogulla from as far away as Kutighat. A minister – no less – was a regular customer. Beekayda was good to everybody. But he treated the ordinary folk of Shyam Bazar as his family. For them, he kept aside a tray of fresh sweets – even though it might go unsold that day. A neighbourhood boy who paid for three cham-cham was bound to leave with four, and an old widow was presented with a mishti doi as she passed by in front of the shop.

The recent rains had washed the red-tiled roofs and greened the gardens. It was such a pretty sight.

Although it was still early in the day, there were children in the playground. They must be happy that the sky had cleared. Some were on the swings, other were playing hopscotch. In Bengali, they called it ekka-dokka – it was a game for girls. A boy could spend hours shooting marbles with his friends or spinning a lattoo, a wooden top, all by himself. When it rained, he and his sister Tuk-tuk played indoors, sometimes ekka-dokka, sometimes lattoo. Their mother would be busy with housework, and they kept out of her way. Morning was always a busy time for mothers.

Miss Riddle did not have a mother. He felt very sorry when he learned this. It must have been difficult for her father to bring her up alone. It was a credit to him that she was such a kind person. Some might say that fate had brought them together, but he did not believe in fate. It could have been pure chance, an accident – he did not see it that way either. Instead, he saw it as a series of choices – of thought, word and deed – that they both had made, neither pre-ordained nor random. He did not know how to explain it. All he knew was that it was magical. The magic was strongest when he was with her, but it stayed even when they were apart. Just knowing that she existed was enough. Her existence gave his a purpose.

Labourers had finished raising the wall on the eastern boundary by two feet. Now they were embedding the top with shards of broken glass. Peter Lazarus was absolutely right. The enemy could strike anywhere, any time. Railway property must be protected at all costs, and so must railway people.

Firing practice took place every morning. More watchmen had been recruited, the number of patrols increased, security at the gates tightened. All that remained was to strengthen the boundary wall of the railway colony. Work on the last stretch had been held up by rain. A week of clear weather would be enough to complete it.

Nobody else was about. Reluctant to replace the binoculars in their case, Chuckerbutty scanned the colony once again. A movement on the southern boundary caught his eye. Usually he paid no attention to that end, though it was right under his nose. Usually there was nothing to see – except a stretch of wasteland leading to the low fence that separated the colony from the barracks. This time, about a dozen labourers were at work – sorting bricks, mixing mortar. Pulling down the bamboo fence. Putting up a wall. A wall that stretched from east to west. And the narrow opening for access to the barracks – always there but never used – had been closed.

Chuckerbutty turned away from the window. There was nothing more for him to see.

Every man was created for a reason. It did not matter whether he was born in a village or a city, whether he was rich or poor. His past only told him where he came from, not where he would go. The path he took was entirely up to him. His existence had a special meaning, a purpose. It could be to lead, or it could be to follow. To teach or to learn. To give or to receive. It was not easy to discover that purpose. In fact, he might never do so. He could go through his entire life without knowing what he was meant for. But if he searched his heart humbly, sincerely, he would know. Knowing was just the first step. Life would take many twists and turns, it would throw many hurdles in his path. It would try him and test him, time and time again. It was only the most fortunate of men who lived to serve their purpose. And it was only the chosen few among them who served others rather than themselves.

There were times when the future of humanity was poised on the brink of destruction. When all the gains of civilisation could have been lost in the blink of an eye, spelling the end of all that was good and noble and just. This was such a time.

35
Kitty

Kitty woke with a start. She did not remember putting a cushion behind her head – her father must have placed it there before going to bed. It had been ages since they sat together after dinner. The last thing she recalled was him playing *The Thieving Magpie*. It must have put her to sleep. She could not have been out for more than an hour, but she slept better than she had that entire week. With its own sense of space, its own speed of time, the verandah was a refuge from the chaos within and without.

Sitting up, she took her feet off the table and picked up the mug of cocoa. She pinched the skin puckered over its face, flicked it away, and took a sip. It tasted ghastly. Beneath her chair, the white dog stirred. A paw brushed against her bare toes. It tickled, but did not offend.

The next minute, the dog shot out from under the chair. She stood perfectly still, front paw raised, ears cocked, nose aquiver. Then she turned her head and looked at

Kitty, her doe-like eyes unblinking. The house was quiet, so was the lane. Kitty fastened her sandals and picked up the small torch that hung on a nail behind the front door. The white dog hurried down the driveway as though the two of them had important business to attend to. She led the way through the gate without stopping to see if Kitty was following. She was, though not without second thoughts. At the end of the street, they ran into Stanley McBride and Jim Adams, who were out on night patrol.

'Dog taking you for a walk?' Jim called out.

'You could say that.'

Stanley emitted a jet of smoke. 'Lovely night, isn't it?'

'Yes,' she agreed, 'yes, it is.' There was neither moon nor stars, but every now and then, a hint of a breeze blew in from the east, bringing with it the smell of rain.

'Don't stay out too long.' That was Jim again.

'No,' she said, 'I won't.'

The white dog turned right and took the first left into one of the back lanes. The servants' quarters on either side were in darkness. Kitty hesitated for a moment. Then she switched on her torch and walked on. Now they were on the street where Pat and Dan lived. It led straight to the playground further up. The white dog trotted past the sandbox, around the swings, and through the trees. The north-east gate to the station was a couple of yards away. Normally it took her ten minutes to get there – this time it took just five.

Bathed in yellow light, the watchman peered at her through the iron grill. 'Miss Riddle?'

'Yes, it's me. Lovely night, isn't it?'

He looked up at the sky and shook his head. 'No, Miss Riddle, too quiet.'

She laughed. 'Can you open this?'

Fumbling with the keys at his belt, he unlocked the gate and held it ajar. Kitty went through and strolled down the platform with the watchman at her heels. It was then that she realised the white dog was gone.

'You can go now,' she said, 'I'll just stay for a bit.'

The watchman looked doubtful, but returned to his post. Closing her eyes, Kitty saw the signal go down, the guard wave his flag, the locomotive appear through a cloud of steam, and the hell that broke loose when it ground to a halt. When she opened her eyes, the train was gone, leaving behind the sticky smell of soot.

Her mind was never more clear. Jonathan had made his choice. Now it was her turn to choose. She chose to step away from the burden of history and the undivided loyalty that it demanded. She chose herself. Not the foreigners who had come to conquer and to quell. Not the community born of early settlers and native women. Not the country of her birth, which was both exile as well as home. She chose to start over, with Jonathan or without him.

A twig snapped. In the hush of the night, it sounded like a gunshot. Kitty waited a while for the watchman to appear. Then she shrugged and shone her torch on the undergrowth behind the railway line. The beam wobbled weakly over bushes and shrubs before it died. She shook the torch and flicked the switch again. A man holding a jerrycan stood frozen on the tracks.

The watchman struggled to unlock the gate as fast as he could. Kitty's hands were trembling as she forced herself to wait. Finally the bolt clanged home and she stepped forward. Brushing aside his anxious apology, she asked his name and where he was from. And his wife's name and where she was from. And how many children they had. The watchman smiled shyly and held up eight fingers. Without waiting to be asked, he told her their names, and how old each of them was.

Men, women and children were running towards the station, shouting at each other to hurry. Her father was not among them. He was watching quietly from the front verandah. Kitty took his hand and led him inside as flames lit up the sky.

www.ingramcontent.com/pod-product-compliance
Lightning Source LLC
LaVergne TN
LVHW041915070526
838199LV00051BA/2627